# In The Arms Of A Gangster
## (Beautiee's Biography)

# In The Arms Of A Gangster (Beautiee's Biography)

BY

TRACY WILSON

http://beautifulpublications.com

Published by
Beautiful Publications LLC
Stratford, CT 06614

**PRINT ISBN: 978-1-7343352-2-4**
**EBOOK ISBN: 978-1-7343352-3-1**

Printed in the United States of America

# Dedication

This book is dedicated to my husband, Bazil J. Osgood.  When I'm in your arms, I'm in my favorite place, I feel loved, I feel safe, and I feel protected.  I love you Bazil.

# Chapter 1

I was completely done. I was psychologically, emotionally, and physically drained. I knew I shouldn't be turning to alcohol, but it was either a drink or a shotgun and since I couldn't get my hands on a shotgun, a drink would have to do. I sat there admiring the glass of amaretto sour in front of me, picked up the cherry, and slid it into my mouth. I closed my eyes, tilted my head back slightly, and imagined the liquor going down my throat, quenching my thirst, and numbing the pain I was in. I opened my eyes and as I reached for the glass, he wrapped his hand around my hand and held the drink with me. "Who are you?" I asked as I watched him pick up the glass and take a sip with both our hands holding it...

"I'm your Thirst Quencher," he answered as we put the glass down, he leaned towards me, and began kissing me slowly and softly, sliding his tongue in my mouth, allowing me to suck the amaretto flavor. I couldn't take my eyes off of him. It was hot inside and out, and I admired the sweat dripping from his chocolate temples. We

1

picked up the glass again and he took another sip, but this time when he leaned in to kiss me he used his tongue to pour the amaretto into my mouth, sliding his tongue in a little deeper, allowing me to suck and swallow. We lifted the glass again and before he could take a sip, I brought the glass to my mouth and gulped the rest of the drink down. He looked at me with such a sad face and turned to leave but before he could, I turned him back towards me, took his face in my hands, and kissed him fully in the mouth, sliding my tongue into his so he could suck the amaretto flavor. We pulled away from kissing and I was relieved to see I changed his mind...

"Who are you?" he asked.

"I'm Beautiee," I answered as I lowered my head.

"Look at me," he whispered as he gently placed his hand under my chin and picked my head up. "What happened?"

"Long story," I answered as I tried to lower my head but couldn't. When I tried to turn my head away from him, he wouldn't allow it.

"Look at me," he whispered as he turned my head to face him. "I've got all night," he said as he looked into my face.

"I don't want to..."

"It's okay... you don't have to," he said as he stood up. "Come with me... please..." he whispered as he held out his hand. I stood up, took his hand, and allowed him to lead me to the elevator. I knew where we were going but I didn't care... I needed to numb the pain I was in and I was going to numb it one way or the other. The way I figured, this way was better than a shotgun. When the elevator doors opened, I realized where I was and started having second thoughts...

"I can't do this," I whispered as I backed up into the elevator. He stood in the door, blocking it from closing...

"Don't leave me Beautiee... please..." he whispered as he extended his hand for me to take. I took his hand again and allowed him to lead me out the elevator down the hall and into his room. Once inside, I looked around the suite, admiring the décor. The master bath was off to the right with two sinks, porcelain countertops, recessed lighting, and marble floors, and a shower built for two. The king size bed was to the left, made up with brown, cream, and red comforters and pillows. In the middle of the room was a chocolate chaise lounge, and to the right of that was a desk with a computer, a lamp, paper, pens, and a phone. "Make yourself comfortable..." he said as he sat down on his bed and patted, motioning for me to sit down next to him...

"I'd like to take a shower," I said as I opened the closet door and took the robe off the hanger.

"Whatever you want," he said, looking at me seductively.

"I need another drink" I said as I walked over to the chaise lounge and sat down.

"Amaretto sour?" he asked.

"I need something a little stronger... something to take the edge off..."

"I'll make you another amaretto," he said, completely ignoring my request. When he sat down on the chaise lounge next to me with the drink, I reached for the drink but he playfully pulled it away, smiling. "Say please..." he commanded.

"Please," I said sarcastically.

"You can do better than that," he replied just as sarcastically.

"Look," I said as I turned to face him.

"Yes Beautiee?" he said as he turned to look at me. I could tell he was really enjoying this...

"Who are you?" I asked.

"I'm your Thirst Quencher," he answered, still holding the drink...

"The ice is beginning to melt... and I'm really thirsty..."

"Here," he said as he handed me the glass and I wrapped my hand around his hand.

"Thank you," I replied, slowly taking a sip and pulling the glass away. He watched me swallow and as we both dropped the glass, he pushed me back onto the chaise lounge and began kissing me forcefully. He slowed down when he sensed I wasn't enjoying it and continued kissing me softly and sensually, sucking my tongue, tasting the amaretto. "MmmmMmmm..." he moaned between kisses, moving from my mouth to my neck...

"Don't..." I whispered...

"Please..." he panted while continuing to kiss my neck...

"I... need..." I tried to explain between kisses...

"You... need... to... let... me... be... your... Thirst... Quencher...

"Shower..." I panted...

"Okay... I'll join you..." I didn't want him to...

"No..." I panted...

"Please..."

"I'll be right back..."

"I'm... coming... with... you..."

"Okay..." I relented.

"Come with me," he said as he stood up and reached for my hand. I took his hand, stood up, picked up the robe, and let him lead me to the shower. I stepped into the bathroom and watched him come up behind me in the mirror. He unzipped my dress and began kissing my neck as he slid my dress off my shoulders and it fell to the floor. He was pleasantly surprised when he saw I was naked underneath. He quickly disrobed, dropping his clothes to the floor, turning me around to face him. His look quickly changed from seductive to hurt when he saw the bruises on my body. I tried to look away but he placed his hand under my chin, turned me to him, pulled me close to him, and kissed me. He reached to turn on the shower, took me by the hand, and led me inside. I stood underneath the water and let it soothe me as he reached for the shampoo, squirting some in his hands. He began to massage my scalp while simultaneously kissing the back of my neck...

"Mmmmmm..... That's nice..." I moaned as I began to relax...

"Ouch... what the... oh my God... Beautiee..." he whispered as he pulled his left hand away to look at the blood. I couldn't turn to look at him. I just continued to stand under the water, facing the wall, until he turned me around to face him... "Beautiee... this is glass... I need to check to see if you're still bleeding... you might need stitches... let me rinse this out... I'll try not to hurt you... be still..." he said as the shampoo ran down my head and face... "Turn your head this way... it looks like you might need stitches...

"No... I said, shaking my head.

"Let's get you cleaned up," he said completely ignoring me, until... "What are you doing?"

"What does it feel like I'm doing?" I asked him as I continued 'washing' his dick.

"It... feels... nice..." he moaned as I continued soaping him up and down. I loved watching the creamy lather run down his chocolate body...

"Ouch," I said as he started soaping my bruises...

"I'm sorry Beautiee," he whispered as he pulled me into a passionate kiss. I could feel his erection against me and I wanted him – needed him. I felt safe and secure in his arms and I wanted to stay in them for as long as I could. We stopped kissing and I wrapped my arms around him as he continued to hold me against him. "Come here," he whispered as he led me out the shower towards the bench. I sat down and he gently towel-dried my hair, being particularly careful on the left side of my head. "It looks like the bleeding stopped... you may not need stitches," he said as he continued to dry me off and then himself. When he was finished he lifted me up off the bench, careful not to grab me by my bruises, carried me to the bed, and gently laid me down on the bed. He lay behind me and pulled me close to him, spooning me, kissing me softly on my neck and shoulder...

"You... feel... so... good...," I yawned as I drifted off the sleep.

# Chapter 2

"Mmmmmm....." I yawned and stretched... "Wait... what the hell... where am I... why am I naked... oh God... what happened last night?" I whispered as I started to cry... then I heard the door...

"Good morning Beautiee," he said as he came into the room with room service.

"Who are you?" I asked.

"I'm your Thirst Quencher," he answered seductively.

"My what?"

"Your Thirst Quencher," he said again as he came towards the bed...

"Why am I naked?"

"You wanted to take a shower," he whispered as he sat down close to me and started kissing me on my neck...

"Wait..."

"No..." he said playfully...

"What happened last night?"

"Here... put this on... let's have some breakfast," he said as he handed me the robe.

"Okay..." When I stood up I saw the bruises in the mirror as I was putting on the robe. I looked at him, put the robe on, and sat down to eat.

"Coffee?"

"Yes... thank you."

"When I saw you, you were in bad shape," he said as he lifted the covers off our plates. We each had scrambled eggs, bacon, home fries, toast, fruit, pastries, and orange juice.

"Where did you see me?" I asked as I ate.

"I saw you at the bar," he answered as he alternated between drinking and swallowing.

"Oh God... was I drinking?"

"Yes."

"How much did I have to drink?"

"Before I saw you... I don't know... but once I sat down and we both held the glass..."

"We both held the glass?"

"Yes..."

"That sounds nice," I said as I finished my food."

"It was... especially when you let me quench your thirst..."

"I did what?"

"We held the glass... I took a sip... I kissed you... and you sucked the amaretto off my tongue..."

"Oh wow..." I whispered, more intrigued and less afraid.

"I led you to the elevator... you didn't want to come at first..."

"How did you convince me?"

"I said please don't leave me... and you didn't..." he answered seductively.

"Is that why I'm naked?"

"No... I made you another drink... you took a sip... we dropped the glass... I started kissing you..."

"Did we make love?"

"No... you wanted to take a shower..."

"Did we make love in the shower?"

"No..."

"Why not?"

"I started to wash your hair... there was glass... there was blood...," he said as he got up and came towards me...

"What are you doing?"

"I'm checking your head," he answered as he ran his fingers through my hair, paying close attention to the left side of my head...

"That hurts," I whispered...

"I'm so sorry Beautiee...," he whispered as he started kissing me on my neck...

"Did you hurt me?" I asked tearfully.

"Beautiee..." he answered with hurt and anguish on his face... "I could never hurt you... I love you..." he answered as he leaned in to kiss me...

"You love me?"

"Yeeesss... Beautiee... I love you..." he moaned as he continued kissing me softly...

"So... who hurt me then?" I asked with tears in my eyes...

"I don't know who hurt you..." he said as he laid me back on the bed, opened my robe, and climbed on top of me... "But I swear on my life... when I find out... he's a fuckin' dead man..." he growled as he spread my legs...

"Don't..." I whispered as he continued kissing me...

"Please... I love you... Don't you want me?"

"I'm scared..."

"I know..."

"Please don't..."

"Okay... I'll stop... if that's what you want..." he panted as he kissed me fully in the mouth while sliding his right hand across my breasts...

"Mmmmm..."

"Do you still want me to stop?" he asked as he slid down and began sucking my right nipple while caressing my left breast...

"Oooohhh...."

"So you don't want me to stop... I didn't think so..." he panted as he began swirling his tongue around my left nipple while caressing my right breast. I lifted my head slightly and started trembling as he slid his hands under the small of my back. Lifting me up...

"I'm scared..."

"Don't be... I won't hurt you... I promise..." he moaned as I felt his breath between my legs...

"You promise?"

"Proommmmmissseeee..."

11

"Ohhh…. Yeeesss…." I moaned as he buried his face between my legs and began licking, sucking, and slurping… "Stop…"

"Am I hurting you?"

"No…"

"Then why?"

"I don't want to cum…"

"Why…" he panted as he slowed down but didn't stop completely…

"Because… I won't cum again…" I breathed…

"I'll make you cum as much as you want…"

"Promise?"

"Promise… now where was I…"

"Ooohhh… right there…"

"Yeesss… right here…"

"Don't stop… I'm cumming!" I screamed as I arched my back up off the bed, trembling as he continued licking, sucking, and slurping…

"Mmmmmm…. You taste delicious…" he said as he stood up and began taking off his clothes. He looked so good standing there completely nude, chiseled in all the right places. He stood there and smiled, allowing me to admire his body, stroking his dick slowly, hypnotizing me. As he approached the bed, I slid down to the edge and hesitated before taking his dick in my mouth…

"Beautiee…" he moaned as I took his dick all the way in my mouth, down my throat, then slowly pulling it back out, swirling my tongue around it as I did so, then taking it back in my mouth again... Stop..."

"Did I do something wrong?" I asked as I looked up at him while continuing to lick his dick...

"No Beautiee... you did everything right," he panted as he pushed me back a little and stood away from me. "Move back, he commanded. I did as I was told and he sat in front of me on the bed, spreading his legs. "Come sit here," he commanded, motioning for me to sit on his dick.

"Oooohhh..." I moaned as I slid onto his dick all the way down to his balls...

"Come here," he commanded as he pulled me close to him and began stroking me, holding me and kissing me passionately...

"Mmmmmm..... Mmmmmm.... Mmmmmm...." I moaned as I squeezed him tighter. He felt so good... his dick was amazing... he was giving me life... and he was making me cum... "Shit..." I moaned as I closed my eyes, tilted my head back, braced myself, and enjoyed the ride...

"Fuck..." he moaned as he squeezed me harder, burying his head in my neck...

"Yyyeeesss..." I moaned, wrapping my arms around his neck...

"I'm cummmmmiiinnng!" he growled...

"I'm cmmmmmiiinnng with you!" I screamed as we came together. We began kissing each other, taking turns sucking each other's tongues, and holding each other as our orgasms transcended from our bodies to our hearts...

"I love you Beautiee..."

"I love you too... Thirst Quencher..."

"I guess I should tell you my name," he laughed.

"Thirst Quencher..." I sighed as I lay my head on his shoulder..."

"Bazil... my name is Bazil..."

"Thirst Quencher..." I repeated as I pulled him into a kiss...

"As... much... as... I'm... enjoying... this..."

"Yyyeeeesss..."

"We... need... to... check... out..."

"I... don't... want... to... check... out..."

"You... want... more..."

"Yyyyeeesss... please..." I breathed as he began thrusting...

"Mmmmmm...."

"Yyyyeesss.... right... there..."

"Oooohhh...."

"Fuck... ooohhhh... sshhhiiittt..." he growled as he grabbed me up and laid me down in one quick motion...

"Oooohhh.... yyeeesss... harder..."

"Is... that... what... you... want?"

"Oooohhh... God.... Yyyeeesssss!" I screamed as he threw my legs up on his shoulders and continued thrusting...

"Uuuggghhh... uuuggghhh... uuuggghhh... uuuggghhh!" We continued to lay there, panting, and kissing for a few minutes...You... got... some... good... pussy..."

"You... got... some... good... dick..." I sighed...

"Indeed..."

"It's... been... so... long..."

"So long for what?" Dick?"

"Yes... and no..."

"What then?"

"It's been so long since I've felt good..."

"It's... been... my... pleasure... to... make... you... feel... better..."

"Mine too..."

"Marry... me... Beautiee..."

"Whhhaaattt???"

"I... said... Marry... me..."

"Wait... are... you... serious?"

"Yeeesss... Beautiee..."

"But... MmmmMmmm..." I moaned as he kissed me deeper, purposely covering my mouth with his, swirling his tongue around mine so I couldn't object..."MmmmMmmmmm..." I moaned as he started thrusting again...

"Mmmmmm....." he moaned as he started thrusting harder and deeper...

"Mmmmmm.....     Mmmmmm..... Mmmmmm....." was all I could do and all I wanted to do as he continued thrusting because he never let up, his mouth was still covering mine, his tongue was still deep inside, and I was cumming again...

"Mmmmmmph...        Mmmmmmph... Mmmmmmph..."

"Mmmmmm...        Mmmmmm... Mmmmmm..."

"Is... that... a.... yes...?"

"I... want... to... but..."

"Beautiee?"

"Yes?"

"You just said it's been a long time since you've felt good right?" he asked as he propped himself on his arm beside me while caressing me...

"Yyyeeesss..."

"So..." we started kissing again... "Marry... me... and... if... you... do... I promise... I'll make you feel good... everyday... for the rest of your life..."

"Okay... I'll... marry... you..."

"Did you just say yes?"

"Yes my Thirst Quencher... I said yes... I'll marry you!"

"Beautiee... I love you..." he whispered with tears in his eyes..."

"I love you too... now let's plan a wedding!" I yelled as I jumped out of bed.

"Easy Beautiee," he laughed as he jumped up out the bed after me and grabbed me from behind, kissing me on my neck..."Go get in the shower... I'll see you when you get out..."

16

"Aren't you coming with me?" I pouted.

"I'd love to join you... but I have something I need to take care of... and I need to do it quickly so we can check outta here on time," he answered as he picked up his cell phone.

"Okay my Thirst Quencher," I said as I ran off to jump in the shower.

# Chapter 3

"Your turn!" I squealed as I ran up behind Bazil and began kissing him on his neck...

"Beautiee... sit down... we need to talk..."

"Is everything okay?" I asked, praying that he wasn't about to change his mind...

"No..."

"What's wrong?"

"I want to give you the most beautiful, romantic wedding your heart desires..."

"I don't care about that my Thirst Quencher..."

"But I do... and I want our wedding day to be special..."

"It will be..."

"While you were in the shower... I was thinking... How would you feel about getting married in Vegas?"

"You're not going to believe this..."

"Believe what?"

"I've always wanted to get married in Vegas..."

"You have?"

"Yes..."

"Well then... I'll go get in the shower... and you sit here... go on the computer... and pick out whatever you want," he said before he pulled me into a kiss...

"Okay my Thirst Quencher," I beamed. I watched him turn to go towards the bathroom and got turned on again by the sight of his ass... "Le'me get on this computer," I said out loud as I turned it on and went to littlechapel.com/wedding-packages. I went to the Chapel of the Flowers and looked at the packages and chose the Cherish package. The silk flower petals, roses, bouquet, and boutonniere were stunning. The package also included photography, a wedding coordinator, a wedding planner, live music, round-trip limousine service for the bride, a separate limousine for the groom, hair and make-up, a VIP Consultation Service to the Reginal Justice Center to obtain your marriage license, and a video of the ceremony. I went to look at the venues and immediately fell in love with the Magnolia Chapel. I was mesmerized by the marble mosaic floors, crystal chandeliers, light gray shimmering wallpaper, crystal beaded curtains, dual glass mirrored silver pillars, elegant candelabras, and custom blush benches with leather finishes. I logged into my account at hotes.com and looked at all the hotels with 5-star ratings. I kept scrolling and clicking... and then I found it... the Four Seasons Hotel. "This is the one," I said out loud as I looked at the pictures of the Presidential Suite. The views of Vegas were breathtaking from all the windows of the room and the master bathroom was the most elegant I'd ever seen. I nearly fell out of my chair when I saw $3,000 per night...

"Hey...," he said as he caught me.

"Hey...," I sighed.

"Find everything you want?"

"Yyyyeeeessss...," I moaned.

"Okay... here... take this," he said as he handed me a Black American Express Card... "and book it while I get dressed..."

"Wait..."

"What's wrong Beautiee?"

"I can't..."

"You can't marry me?"

"Yes... I can marry you... but..."

"Come here Beautiee," he said as he patted the bed for me to sit next to him. "Talk to me...," he pleaded.

"I can't wear that dress..."

"The dress from last night?"

"Yea..."

"Here... put this on... I hope you like it... it's all I could find on short notice," he said as he handed me the bag and I took out the clothes..."

"Oooohhh... I hope these fit me..."

"If they don't, we'll go get you something that fits," he smiled.

"Okay," I squealed as I jumped up off the bed and reached for the red underwear. I loved the way he was looking at me as I put them on.

"They look good on you," he said seductively.

"They feel good too," I said just as seductively.

"Let me help you with that," he said as I tried to reach for the bra. I stood still as he came up behind me and held the bra for me to put my arms through the straps and as he got closer to my shoulders, he began messaging my breasts while kissing me on the back of my neck...

"Oooohhh... that feels so good... my Thirst Quencher...," I moaned as he moved up to my earlobe while continuing to massage my breasts...

"Let me close this for you," he said as he pulled up the straps and clasped the bra. "Perfect," he said lovingly.

"These fit perfectly... how did you know my size?" I asked as I pulled up the jeans..."

"I got to know your body intimately," he answered as he pulled me into a kiss...

"Mmmmmm...," I moaned...

"Here," he said as he pulled the blue shirt over my head and pulled it down.

"Thank you," I whispered.

"You're welcome... put on the socks and sneakers," he said as he picked up the phone...

"Yes... we need a later check out... 3pm... okay... thanks...

"What about my hair?" I asked.

"Let me look at you," he said as he ran his fingers through my hair... "Does it still hurt?"

"A little..."

"Leave your hair down then... Let's get this booked... we can leave tonight..."

"Tonight?"

"Yes Beautiee... if that's okay with you..."

"Yyyyeeesssss...," I sighed.

"Good... let's do this," he said as he sat down beside me and looked at my choices..."Oh wow... this is really beautiful... I had no idea..."

"Me either..."

"I can't wait to marry you Beautiee..."

"I can't wait either my Thirst Quencher...," I sighed.

"Okay... it's all set... we just need to book our flight..."

"Can we go first class?"

"Of course... let me see," he said as he was looking at priceline.com..."Perfect... this flight leaves at a little after 10 tonight and we can be in Vegas tomorrow morning..."

"Okay...," I sighed.

"Done! Let's go Beautiee," he said as he opened the door for me...

"Wait... your card..." I said as I ran back to pick it up, looked at it, and read his full name: Bazil J. Osgood.

# Chapter 4

Once we got to the airport and went through check in, I was elated to get on the plane. It was a breeze because we were only wearing what we had on and we had no luggage to check in. Bazil tried peeking over my shoulder without being obvious, but it didn't work...

"What are you looking at Beautiee," he asked me, as if he didn't already know what I was doing...

"What size are you?"

"What size do you think I am...," he asked seductively...

"I'm not talking about your dick," I laughed...

"Well shit... I am... what size are ya?" she laughed. I could tell she had a few too many so I wasn't going to get into a confrontation... but I was definitely going to answer her question...

"He's about the size of this bottle here... would you like to feel it or you gonna take my word for it?"

"Shittt... I ain't had no dick in a while... I might wanna feel that shit," she laughed...

"As you wish!" I said as I stood up and swung the bottle... right into Bazil's hand...

"Give me that," he laughed...

"Get your lady," she laughed...

"See... I was trying to be a gentleman... you know what... never mind... here Beautiee... handle your business!" he said as he handed me back the bottle...

"Well Bitch... whatchu' goin' do?" she slurred...

"I'ma handle my business... like he said," I laughed as I put the bottle down, reached between Bazil's legs, and started massaging his dick...

"Awww shit... y'all 'bout to be in the mile high club," she laughed...

"You wanna?" Bazil asked...

"Hell yea!" I said as we got up out our seats, went into the bathroom, and locked the door... "Drop your pants," I panted... Bazil didn't hesitate... "This is gonna be good," I said as I took his dick in my hand... "But it has to be quick," I said as I started sucking...

"Beautiee...," he moaned as he ran his fingers through my hair before grabbing the sides of my head, pushing his dick further into my mouth... "Oh shit... I'm about to bust my nut... Beautiee...," he moaned as he shot his creamy goodness into the back of my throat... "Easy... I'm a little sensitive..."

"Okay...," I whispered...

"Drop those pants... and bend over...," he commanded. As soon as I did as I was told, he slid inside me and I had to brace myself on the sink to keep from falling... "Bazil... Bazil... Bazil...," I panted as he grabbed a hold of my waist and began thrusting harder and deeper...

"Cum for me Beautiee...," he growled...

"Bazil...," I panted, turning on the blower to muffle our sounds...

"Cum for meeee...," he growled, covering my mouth...

"MmmmMmmmMmmmMmmmmm!" I screamed into his hand while his creamy goodness ran down my legs...

"Everything okay in there?" the stewardess asked as she knocked on the door...

"Everything's fine!" I answered as we cleaned ourselves up, made ourselves presentable, and went back to our seats...

"Congratulations," the stewardess whispered in my year...

"Thank you," I laughed... "Now... what size are you?" I asked Bazil...

"I'm a size 13..."

"Okay," I said as I completed my purchase of the Modern Prong Wedding Band in 14k White Gold from zoara.com. Bazil completed his purchase of the Elegant Shared Prong Diamond Wedding Ring in 14k White Gold for me as I drifted off to sleep. When we woke up, it was time for us to get off the plane so we got up out our seats, waited for the stewardess to open the door, and we walked off hand-in-hand. After we got our bags, we got in the limousine, and went straight to City Hall.

# Chapter 5

"Good afternoon..." the clerk smiled... "How may I help you?"

"We're here to get our marriage license..." I said as I smiled...

"Aww... congratulations..."

"Thank you..."

"Do you have valid identification?"

"We have valid identification..." Bazil said as he showed the clerk his driver's license...

"May I have your ID please?" she asked me...

"Sure..." I said as I handed her my license...

"I need to make a copy of these to attach to your application – I'll be right back..." she said as she walked over to the copy machine. Bazil and I looked at each other and smiled...

"Here ya go..." the clerk said as she gave us back our licenses...

"I need you both to fill this out completely – once you fill it out – I'll look it over, make sure it's filled out properly, and then we'll all sign it..."

"Okay…" Bazil said as he took the form and began filling it out. I waited patiently as he filled out his side, but I wanted him to hurry up so I could fill out mine…

"Here, here!" Bazil laughed as he gave it to me. I studied his side and then started filling out my side with my name, date of birth, social security number, etc., and then I filled in the rest of the form: Mother – Connie Thompson, Father – Jake Thompson, City of Birth – Mt. Vernon, State – NY, Prior Marriages – No, Maiden Name – Beautiee Thompson, Name on Marriage Certificate –Beautiee Osgood

After I filled in the name to be put on the Marriage Certificate I checked 'no' where they asked for preference to hyphenate the name. I saw Bazil's signature at the bottom of the form and I started crying after I signed my name…

"Aww…" the clerk said as she handed me tissues…

"Sorry…" I laughed…

"Don't ever apologize for happiness…" she said as she took the form and read it over…

"Bazil?" she asked…

"Yes?"

"Did you fill this out of your own free will?"

"Yes Maam…"

"Is this your signature?" she asked as she pointed to his signature…

"Yes Maam…"

"Beautiee?"

28

"Yes?"

"Did you fill this out of your own free will?"

"Yes Maam!"

"Is this your signature?" she asked as she pointed to my signature...

"Yes Maam!"

"Okay..." she laughed as she signed the form. "I'm going to process this and get you your license – once I do that – you can get married - I'll be right back..." she said as she went into the office behind the counter...

"I love you Bazil..."

"I love you too..." Bazil said and then he kissed me...

"Here's your license..." the clerk said as she handed us our license. We looked at the license, and then we looked at each other...

"Do you have any questions?" I looked at our license again and read the signature at the bottom:

Prepared by: Roselle DeNino
Title:        City Clerk
City:         Las Vegas
State:        NV

"No..." I sighed...

"Do you have any questions Bazil?"

"No Maam..."

"After you get married I'll sign it, date it, and then I'll mail it out to Vital Records for

Nevada. You'll receive your Marriage Certificate from the Vital Records Office..."

"Thank you Ms. DeNino..." I said as I gave her a hug..."

"You can call me Roselle..." she said as she pulled us both into a hug and started crying...

"You okay?" Bazil asked...

"I'm fine – I'm just happy..." she said as she wiped her eyes..."

"Aww... we're happy too... right Beautiee?"

"Yessss..." I breathed...

"Okay – I'm going to head on over to the Magnolia Chapel – I'll see you soon..." Roselle said as she left. We went outside, got back in the limousine, and headed to Kay Jewelers...

Bazil got out, extended his hand, helped me out, and we both went inside...

"Good afternoon – welcome to Kay Jewelers – my name is Jack - how may I help you?"

"We're here to pick up our wedding rings..." Bazil answered...

"May I please have your name?"

"Bazil Osgood..."

"Mr. Osgood! We've been expecting you – you're here to pick up the Modern Prong Wedding Band in 14k White Gold and the Elegant Shared Prong Diamond Wedding Ring in 14k White Gold – right?"

"Yes – that's right..."

"Come with me..." Jack said as he came out from behind the counter and escorted Bazil behind the counter and into the back room. I waited for them to come out and Jack put the rings on the counter in their boxes so we could see them in the light...

"Beautiee... what do you think?" I didn't answer him... I took his face in my hands and kissed him hard...

"Oh my – you must really love your rings!" Jack laughed...

"I really love our rings... and I really love him..." I said as Bazil smiled...

"You wanna try them on?"

"I dunno..." I sighed...

"Why not?" Bazil asked...

"I might not want to take it off..."

"I understand – we have another set in the case over here if you'd like to see how it'll look on your hand...

"No – I wanna try on our rings!" I squealed...

"Changed your mind huh?" Bazil laughed...

"Yea..." I sighed...

"Give me your hand..." Bazil said. I gave him my hand and I started shaking as he put the ring on my finger...

"It's perfect..." I sighed as I looked at my hand...

"It looks really great on you..." Jack said...

31

"Give me your hand Bazil..." I said. Bazil gave me his hand and I took my time putting the ring on his finger...

"Beautiee..." he breathed as he kissed me...

"You like it?"

"I love it... you have exquisite taste..."

"I agree – you do have exquisite taste – maybe I'll be so blessed one day..." Jack said...

"You will..." I said...

"From your lips to God's ears – let me get these in a bag for you so you can go get married – congratulations!"

"Thank you..." we both said in unison. Bazil took the bag, took my hand, we got back in the limousine, and headed straight to David's Bridal...

Bazil got out, extended his hand, helped me out, and we both went inside...

"Good afternoon – welcome to David's Bridal – my name is Jessica – how may I help you?"

"We're here to pick up my tuxedo and her wedding dress..." Bazil answered...

"Congratulations! May I have your names?"

"Thank you – I'm Bazil Osgood and this is Beautiee..."

"Mr. Osgood – we've been waiting for you to get here – would you like to try on your tuxedo?"

"Do we have time?"

"We'll make time…"

"I don't wanna be late for our wedding…" I sighed…

"Where are you getting married?"

"At the Magnolia Chapel…"

"Oh don't worry – they won't start without you – I'll call Roselle and let her know you're here…"

"Thank you Jessica – I appreciate it…"

"I know you're in a hurry – I just wanna make sure everything fits perfectly…"

"What if it doesn't?" Bazil asked…

"We have what you ordered in stock – if it doesn't fit, we'll just re-size you…"

"Thank you Jessica…"

"You're welcome – Beautiee – I'm going to ask you to wait here – okay?"

"Okay… I guess…"

"I don't want you to see him before the wedding – and I don't want him to see you either…"

"Oh – okay!" I squealed…

"C'mon Mr. Osgood – I can see how excited she is!" Jessica laughed as she took Bazil in the back.  I sat down and waited for about 15 minutes or so and then I saw them heading to the front with a couple of bags…

"Ohhh… can I see?" I asked…

"No…" Bazil answered as he pulled me into a kiss and held the bag away from me…

"Okay…" I sighed…

"C'mon Beautiee – let's go get you into your gown – we'll be right back…" Jessica said as she took me by the hand and we hurried to the back… "Your dress is already in the dressing room – go try it on – I'll come in when you're ready…"

"You can come in now if you want…" I said…

"You want me to come in? Now?"

"Yea…"

"Okay – sure…" Jessica smiled as she came in the dressing room with me…

"I can't believe I'm doing this…" I sighed as I took off my clothes and put on the dress…

"You're not sure you wanna marry him?"

"Hell yea I'm sure – but we've only known each other since last night…"

"What? Oh my God!"

"We met last night at the hotel… I went to his room… we took a shower together… and then we went to sleep…"

"Aww… that sounds nice…"

"He asked me to marry him this morning after we made love… and I said yes…"

"Aww… that's beautiful…" she said as she started crying…

"This dress... is beautiful... too..." I said as I cried...

"Okay... c'mon... we'll never get you outta here like this..." she laughed as we hugged each other...

"I can't wait for him to see me in this dress..." I sighed...

"I'm so happy for you... thank you for sharing with me..."

"You're welcome..." I said as she helped me take off the dress and we put it in a bag...

"Okay – we're ready – let's go up-front to your husband..." she said as she took the bag, took me by the hand, and we hurried to the front of the store... "Everything you need is in there – congratulations – now go get married!"

"Okay..." Bazil laughed as he took my hand, we went outside, got back in the limousine, and headed straight for the Magnolia Chapel...

"Thank God – c'mon!" the stylist said as she took me by the hand and led me away from Bazil into another room...

"C'mon Mr. Osgood..." the 2nd stylist said as he took Bazil by the hand and led him into the other room...

"Beautiee – we're gonna get you dressed – and then we'll do your hair and make-up..." the stylist said as she took my dress, shoes, etc. out the bag...

"I'm going to do your hair and make-up..." another stylist said as she came over to me, held up my face by my chin, turned my head left and right, and went over to the make-up...

"Go light on the make-up..." I said...

"Good idea – less is more – especially 'cause you're already pretty..." she said as she looked through the different foundations...

"Aww... thank you..."

"You're welcome – take off your clothes..."

"Okay..." I laughed as I got up, took my clothes off, and sat back in the chair...

"How would you like to wear your hair?"

"I'd like to wear it down..."

"Okay – I'll give you some curls to accentuate your face..." she said as she styled my hair and put in the Classic Pave Crystal Floral Comb... "How's this?" she asked...

"I love it..." I whispered as I started crying...

"Uh uh – we can't have that – you can't cry until after I've done your make-up – and make sure you dab with tissues – don't wipe – you don't wanna smear your make-up – we need you to look good for your pictures..."

"Okay..." I sniffed. I sat still until I finished my make-up and then I got up to look in the mirror...

"Is that light enough for you?"

"Yes... thank you..."

"You're welcome...Congratulations..." she said as she started to leave...

"Wait..."

"Yes?"

"What's your name?"

"Linda..."

"Thank you Linda..."

"You're welcome..." she said as she left...

"Ready for me now?" the 1st stylist laughed...

"Yesss....." I breathed...

"Okay – let's get you dressed..." she said as she helped me put on my Floral Beaded Lace & Tule Mermaid dress. Once I got my dress on she helped me step into my Pearlized Platform Sandals with Scalloped Edges...

"Oh my God..." I whispered...

"Uh uh – stop that – you don't have any tissues!" she laughed...

"You're right – what's your name?"

"Lori..."

"Thank you Lori..."

"You're welcome – wait here..." she said as she left the room...

"Okay Beautiee – let's go!" Lori said as she extended her arm so she could escort me down the aisle. I could hear the orchestra playing, 'So Nice To Be With You' by Smokey Robinson on violins and I started to cry...

"Uh uh – you don't have any tissues!" Lori whispered as she handed me a tissue and I dabbed my eyes and walked into the room...

"Beautiee..." Bazil whispered as I started walking down the aisle. I tried not to cry but I couldn't help it. When I got to where Bazil was standing, Bazil took my face in his hands, kissed me, pulled me close to him, and we started dancing... "I love you..." Bazil whispered as tears streamed down his face...

"I love you too..."

"You look beautiful..."

"So do you..."

"I can't believe we're getting married..."

"Neither can I..." Roselle and Lori watched as we looked into each other's eyes and danced until the song was over. When the orchestra stopped playing we started kissing...

"Beloved..." Roselle laughed as she interrupted us... "We are gathered here this afternoon to join Beautiee Thompson and Bazil Osgood in marriage. You have both come before me and expressed your desire to become husband and wife. Do you have rings?"

"Yes – we have rings..." Bazil said as he took two ring boxes out his pocket...

"Okay – take the rings out the boxes – Beautiee – you take his ring – Bazil – you take her ring..."

"Okay..." we both said in unison as I took his ring and he took mine...

"Okay – Beautiee – do you have anything you want to say to Bazil?"

"Yes I do..." I answered as I took his hands... "Bazil... my Thirst Quencher... my love... if anyone ever told me that not only would I meet the love of my life, but that I'd also be marrying him... I wouldn't have listened to them or believed them," I said as I started to tear up... "You saw me at my worst and chose me in spite of what you saw... you comforted me... you loved me... and you made me feel something I haven't felt in a long time... you made me feel good. When you came to me... you gave me life and you saved my life... I love you sooo much... and I promise to love you forever," I said as I cried. Bazil didn't wait for Roselle to ask as he responded to me...

"Beautiee... my love... I've been looking for you forever," Bazil said as he teared up... "And I never thought I'd find you," he said as he broke down crying. Roselle was crying along with us both as she handed us tissues. After Bazil composed himself he continued... "I knew I loved you from the moment I saw you... even in your darkest place you were beautiful to me... I know I'm your Thirst Quencher... but Beautiee... you are also my Thirst Quencher," he said as he started tearing up again... "When you chose me you also gave me life and saved my life... I love you Beautiee... thank you for choosing me," he said as he cried...

"Bazil – put the ring on Beautiee's finger – and repeat after me..."

"Okay – I'm ready..." Bazil said...

"Beautiee – I take you as my wife, with your faults and your strengths, as I offer myself to you with my faults and my strengths..." Bazil repeated after Roselle and then she continued... "I will help you when you need help and turn to you when I need help. Today - I choose to spend the rest of my life with you..." I started crying as Bazil repeated the vows to me. When he was finished, I took his face in my hands and kissed him... Roselle waited for us to finish kissing and then she continued...

"Okay Beautiee – put the ring on Bazil's finger - and repeat after me..."

"Okay – I'm ready..." I said...

"Bazil... My Thirst Quencher..." I said... and then I started crying. Bazil took his hands, touched my face, and started crying as I continued... "I take you as my husband, with your faults and your strengths, as I offer myself to you with my faults and my strengths. I will help you when you need help and turn to you when I need help. Today – I choose to spend the rest of my life with you..."

"I love you so much Beautiee..." Bazil
breathed as he kissed me hard...

"I love you too..."

"By the power invested in me by the State
of Nevada – I now pronounce you husband and
wife!" Roselle said as Bazil pulled me to him and
we held each other, kissing feverishly...
"Ummmm... your limousine is waiting to take
you back to your hotel..." she laughed...

"I love you Mrs. Osgood..."

"I love you Mr. Osgood..."

"I can't wait to get back to the hotel..."

"Neither can I..."

"We'll be in touch with you when your
video and pictures are ready..."

"Thank you – come with me Mrs. Osgood!"
Bazil said as he took me by the hand, escorted me
out to the limousine, made sure I got in, and got
in beside me. We started kissing again and didn't
stop until we got to the hotel...

"We're here..." the driver said...

"Come with me Mrs. Osgood..." Bazil said
as he opened the door, got out, and extended his
hand to help me out the limousine...

"Coming Mr. Osgood..." I beamed as I took
his hand and got out.

"Congratulations!" the driver said as he
took off. Bazil took my hand and we walked into
the hotel lobby to the elevator and took the
elevator to the Presidential Suite. When we got

off the elevator, I started to walk but Bazil stopped me...

"Wait a minute..." he said as he opened the door to the room... "Come here..." he said as he picked me up, carried me into the room, and laid me on the bed... "Welcome to Vegas Mrs. Osgood..." he said as he lay down on top of me and began kissing me fully...

"Mmmm..." I moaned as he moved down to my neck and shoulders...

"Beautiee..." he breathed in my ear as he slid my dress down my body...

"Oh Bazil..." I moaned as he took my breasts in his hands and began licking and sucking my nipples. I ripped his shirt open and grabbed his back, digging my nails into his lower back as he moved down to my stomach. He stood up, slid the dress off me, and looked at me lovingly while taking off his clothes. I watched him get completely naked and he stood there for a few moments, allowing me to admire his gorgeous erection, before he walked towards me...

"Thirsty?" he breathed...

"Yes my Thirst Quencher..." I answered as I pulled him closer so his erection could reach my mouth...

"Beautiee..." he moaned as I took him into my mouth completely, looking up at him to make sure he was watching me, and he was...

"I'm thirsty too..." he moaned before pulling out of my mouth and climbing on top of me...

"Bazil..." I moaned as he slid inside me...

"Yes... Beautiee..." Bazil moaned as he started thrusting...

"Ohh... Ohh... Ohh... Bazil..." I moaned as he started thrusting deeper...

"Ummph... Ummph... Ummph... Ummph..." Bazil moaned as I spread my legs wider and grabbed his back, pushing him in deeper...

"Mmmm... Mmmm... Mmmm..." I moaned in Bazil's mouth as he smothered me with deep kisses...

"Mmmph... Mmmph... Mmmph..." Bazil moaned in my mouth as he braced himself up with his hands and continued thrusting...

"Oh shit... Bazil... I'm cumming..."

"I'm cumming with you..."

"Bazil..."

"Beautiee..."

"Bazil..."

"Beautiee... Uuuggghhhh!"

"Baaazzziiilll!" I screamed as he thrust harder...

"Damn Beautiee..." he breathed as he laid down on top of me and kissed me... "You want more... don't you?"

"Yes Bazil... yes... but let's go in front of the window..."

"Okay..." Bazil breathed as he got up, picked me up, and carried me to the window... "What do you want?" he asked as he bent me over, kissing me down my back...

"I want you Bazil..." I breathed..."

"Here? In front of the window?"

"Yes Bazil... Yes..." I breathed as he slid inside me again... "Bazil... Oh God!" I moaned as I braced myself on the window sill and Bazil grabbed me by my waist as he continued thrusting...

"Is this what you want?"

"Yes Bazil..." I moaned...

"Oh shittt... damn..." Bazil breathed...

"Fuck me Bazil...Oooohhh!"

"Uuugh! Uuugh! Uuugh!" Bazil growled as he slowed down, kissing me on my neck...

"Bazil..."

"Beautiee..." Bazil breathed as I felt his cum dripping down my legs. Bazil stopped, pulled out of me, turned me to face him, and held me... "I love you Mrs. Osgood..." he said as he kissed me...

"I love you too Mr. Osgood..." I said as I kissed him back...

"Come with me..." Bazil said as he took my hand and led me to the shower. Bazil turned on the water, and then came up behind me. We both admired our bodies in the mirror as it steamed up, and then Bazil started kissing me...

"Let's get in the shower..." I said as we moved into the shower while continuing to kiss...

"Mmmm..." Bazil moaned as he reached between my legs and began playing with my pussy while continuing to kiss me...

"Mmmm..." I moaned as I reached down to grab his dick... "Wait..." I breathed as I pushed Bazil away so I could sit down on the bench. After I sat down, I pulled Bazil towards my mouth again and began sucking him as the water beat down on us...

"Oh Beautiee..." Bazil moaned as he began massaging my head through my hair with his hands, steadying himself so he wouldn't come out my mouth. I could tell he was about to cum as his legs started trembling and he grabbed my head, pushing his dick further down my throat... "Aaaagggghhhh!" he yelled as I swallowed his warmth... "Easy Beautiee..." Bazil panted. I slowed down but didn't stop right away. When I did stop, I pulled him to my face by his ass and looked up at him as he looked down at me while playing with my hair... "Cumere..." he said as he pulled me up to stand in front of him... "Hold on..." he commanded as I grabbed the bars on both sides of the bench. Bazil squatted down so his face was directly in front of my pussy, placed my legs on his shoulders, and buried his face in my pussy...

"Oh Bazil..." I moaned as he slid his tongue in and out...

"Bazil... Bazil..." I moaned as he moved his tongue under the hood of my clit... "Bazil... Bazil... Bazil..." I moaned as Bazil started sucking my clit ferociously... "Bazil... I'm cumming... I'm cumming... I'm cumming!" Bazil continued sucking and slurping as my legs shook and clamped around his head...

"Mmmm..." Bazil moaned as he let my legs down...

"Bazil..." I moaned as he pulled me into a kiss and slid inside me before I realized he was erect again... "Ooohhh..." I moaned as I wrapped my arms around his upper body to brace myself...

"Ummph... Ummph... Ummph..." Bazil growled as he grabbed my upper body, pulled me closer, and continued thrusting...

"I'm cumming again... Oooohhhhh...."

"Ummph! Ummph! Ummph!" Bazil growled as he buried his head in my neck...

"Ohh... Ohh... Ohh... Baazziilll!!"

"Aaaaggghhhh!" Bazil growled as we both came..."

"Beautiee..." Bazil moaned in my ear...

"Bazil..." I moaned as I pulled him into a kiss...

"Mmmm... Yesss..."

"We better hurry up and finish before they run out of hot water..." I laughed...

"Okay..." Bazil agreed as we got got out the shower, put on our robes, and walked hand-in-hand back to the bedroom...

"I'm hungry..." I breathed...

"Give me a minute..." Bazil laughed...

"I need to eat..."

"Ooohhh... Okay... let's look at the menu..." he said as he went over to the table, picked up the menu, and sat on the bed... "Hmmm... let's start with the Antipasto Assorted Cheese, Charcuterie Meats..."

"Okay..." I agreed as I sat down on the bed next to him, took his dick in my hand, and started stroking it...

"Mmmm... that feels nice..."

"It does..."

"We can also get a cheese plate – Artisanal Cheeses with Seasonal Accompaniments..." he breathed...

"Mmmm... that sound's good..." I breathed as he got harder in my hand and I continued stroking him...

"That feels... good..." he breathed...

"What else can we get to eat?"

"This... looks... good..." he panted...

"What?"

"Two Tuxedo Strawberries..."

"Le'me see..." I breathed as I continued stroking his dick and he showed me the menu...

"I want the Double Chocolate Brownies and Blondie Cake Pops..."

"Mmmm.... Shit... Okay..."

"Ooohhh. Let's get the Sin City Angus Burger – it comes with Bacon, Avocado, and White Cheddar – and Fries..."

"Okay – that's it!" Bazil growled as he turned around, grabbed me by my shoulders, flipped me on my back, spread my legs, and thrust himself inside me...

"Bazil... Huh... Huh..."

"Uggh! Uggh! Uggh!"

"Huh! Huh! Huh!"

"Uggh! Uggh! Uggh!"

"Huh! Huh! Huh!!"

"Uggh! Uggh! Uggh!"

"Fuck me... I'm cumming... I'm cumming..."

"Uggh! Uggh! Uggh! Uuuggghhhh!" Bazil collapsed on me and kissed me hard...

"Mmmmm..." I moaned as I opened my mouth and we started tonguing each other down...

"I'm going to order room service now..."

"Okay..." I breathed as we continued kissing...

"We'll eat in our dining room..."

"Okay..."

"When we're done eating... we'll go sit in the living room..."

"Okay..."

"And I'll make you an Amaretto Sour..."

"Okay..."

"And... after you drink it... I'll suck your tongue..."

"Huh... Okay..."

"Let me go Beautiee..."

"No..." I breathed as he tried to get up but I locked my legs behind him...

'Okay..." he said as he reached over and picked up the phone...

"Room Service..."

"Hello... I'd like to place an order..." he said as I pulled him back down and kissed his neck...

"Yes Mr. Osgood – what can we get you?"

"Mm mm..." Bazil moaned as I grabbed his ass and pushed him back inside me... "I'll have the Antipasto Assorted Cheese and Charcuterie Meats..."

"Okay..."

"I'll also... have... the Artisanal Cheeses with Seasonal Accompaniments..."

"Okay..."

"Uggh..." Bazil moaned as he started stroking me slowly... "Two Tuxedo Strawberries..."

"Okay..."

"Uggh... Double Chocolate Brownies and Blondie Cake Pops..."

"Okay – anything else?"

"Yeesss... two Sin City Burgers..."

"Okay Mr. Osgood – it'll be about 45 minutes – is that alright?"

"That's fine..." he grunted as he hung up and then started thrusting harder and faster...

"Oohh... Oohh... Oohh... Oohh..."

"Uggh! Uggh! Uggh! Uggh!"

"Damn Bazil... you're fuckin' me so good... huh..."

"Uggh! Uggh! Uggh! Uggh!"

"Fuck me Bazil..."

"Uggh!"

"Aahh!"

"Uggh!"

"Aahh!"

"Uggh!"

"Aahh!"

"Uggh!"

"Aahh!"

"Uuuggghhhh!"

"Aaaaaahhhhhh!"

"Mrs. Osgood..." he breathed as he kissed me...

"Yes... my Thirst Quencher?"

"Is this what I have to look forward too?" he asked as we continued kissing...

"Mmmm... Hmmm..."

"Mmmmm..." he moaned...

"Bazil..." I breathed...

"Yesss... Beautiee..."

"Can... we... talk?" I asked between kisses...

"Yes... we... can... talk..."

"Bazil... stop..."

"No..." he breathed as he pushed his tongue in my mouth...

"Mmmmm...."

"Mmmmm..." Bazil moaned as he climbed on top of me... spread my legs... and I pushed him off me gently...

"Beautiee... you don't want me?"

"Hell yea... I want you..."

"Then why..."

"Because... I can't..." I tried to say as he climbed back on top of me and started kissing me again... "I want... to... talk..."

"Okay... we'll talk... and then..." he breathed in my ear as he kissed my neck and shoulders... "we're fucking..." he said as he started kissing me again... "Do you understand?"

"Yes... Yes my Thirst Quencher..." I breathed as he kissed me fully...

"Okay..." he said as he turned on his side, propped himself up on his elbow, and looked down at me... "Let's talk..."

"I love you..."

"I love you too..."

"Can I ask you something?"

"Of course..."

"I've never felt like this..." Bazil smoothed my hair away from my face and smiled...

"I know..."

"You're so good..."

"I know..."

"We're you always this good?" Bazil bust out laughing...

"Aaahaaaa! Aaahaaaa! Aaahaaaa!"

"I shouldn't've asked..."

"Beautiee..." he laughed... I'm not laughing at you... but..." he said as he laughed again... "I just can't believe you asked me that!" he laughed...

"I'm sorry..."

"Don't be sorry..."

"Okay..."

"I started having sex when I was 16..."

"Okay..."

"My father and I had open communication when it came to sex..."

"That's good..."

"My father told me the key to getting pussy was simple..."

"He did?"

"He said all I had to do was listen..."

"That's it?"

"My father told me listening was the best thing I could do if I wanted pussy – mind you – I was only 16 at the time – so I wasn't sure what he meant – so I asked him what he meant..."

"What'd he say?" I asked as I propped myself up on my elbow...

"My father asked me if I ever heard him having sex with my mother..."

"Really?"

"I told him I heard them sometimes and he asked me what I heard..."

"Oh my God! What'd you say?"

"I told him I heard moaning..."

"You weren't embarrassed?"

"I was – but my father said it was okay to be embarrassed – and then he asked me what I thought when I heard them moaning..."

"What'd you say?"

"I told him I thought it must feel good and he said that's exactly the point - when you're having sex, you listen to her moaning – if she's moaning, that means she's enjoying it – and as long as you make sure she's enjoying it you'll always get pussy..."

"What was your first time like?"

"It was awkward – but she didn't know that..."

"She didn't?"

"Nope – I just remembered what my father said, took my time, and got the pussy..."

"I wish I was that girl..." I sighed...

"I wish you were that girl too..." he breathed as he kissed me..."

"My husband never made me come..."

"Oh shit! Never?"

"Never..."

"So you didn't enjoy it?"

"I enjoyed it up until he came..."

"That's selfish..."

"As soon as I started coming he would come... and then he'd go to sleep..." I sighed...

"Did he ever go down on you?"

"No..."

"Did you suck his dick?"

"Yea..."

"Selfish mutha fucka..."

"When was the first time you ate pussy?"

"In my 20's – when was the first time you sucked dick?"

"I sucked my boyfriend's dick in high school..."

"I wish I was your boyfriend in high school..." Bazil sighed...

"Me too..."

"You ever do 69?"

"No..."

"You wanna do 69?"

"Yea..."

"You wanna be on top?"

"No..."

"You sure?"

"Yea..." I breathed as Bazil ran his hand down my body, between my legs, and spread my lips...

"Ooohhh..." I moaned...

"You're wet..."

"Yeesss..." I moaned as he slid his fingers in and started swirling them around...

"Oooohhh..." I moaned again. Bazil got up on his knees, came towards my head, straddled my head, and put his dick in my mouth. I opened my mouth a bit more, lifted my head a little, and started sucking...

"Oh shit... Beautiee..." Bazil moaned before he held my legs apart and dove in...

"MMMMM! MMMMM! MMMMM!" I moaned on his dick as my body shook and I began experiencing multiple orgasms...

"MMMPH! MMMPH! MMMPH!" Bazil moaned as he quickened his pace and began fucking my mouth harder as his body trembled and I grabbed his ass and squeezed it...

"MMMMMMMMMM!" I moaned on his dick as I arched my back and rose up off the bed...

"MMMMMPPPHH!" Bazil moaned as he came in my mouth and I held him by his ass as I swallowed...

"MMMMM... MMMMM... MMMMM..." I moaned on Bazil's dick as he continued licking, sucking, and slurping, giving me mini orgasms...

"Yes Beautiee... suck it... shit..." he moaned as he started fucking my mouth again and went back to licking, sucking, and slurping while turning me on my side...

"HMMMM... HMMMM... HMMMM... HMMMM... HMMMM..." I moaned as my legs trembled and I came again...

"MMMPH! MMMPH! MMMPH! MMMPH! MMMPH!" Bazil moaned as I pushed his dick in deeper, swallowed, and sucked harder.

Bazil and I let go of each other and lay on our backs as I panted...

"That... was... so... fucking... good!"

"Yes... it... was... intense..."

"I... came... so... hard..."

"Me... too..." Bazil said as he turned himself right-side up and propped himself up on his elbow beside me...

"I loved that..." I breathed...

"So did I..."

"Can we do it again?"

"We can do it..." he said as he kissed me... "As much... as... you... want..."

"Somebody's at the door..." I said as I sat up...

"Hold on!" Bazil said as he jumped up, threw on his robe, and went to the door...

"Room Service!"

"Come on in..." Bazil said as the server came in with the serving cart...

"Shall I put this on the table for you?"

"No thank you..."

"Please sign here..."

"Okay..."

"Congratulations..."

"Thank you... good night..." Bazil said as he closed the door and came back into the bedroom... "Mrs. Osgood – please come with me..."

"Yes Mr. Osgood..." I beamed as I got up outta bed. Bazil held open the robe for me so I could put it on and then he pulled me into a kiss...

"I love you Mrs. Osgood..."

"I love you too..." I breathed. Bazil let go of me, took me by the hand, led me into the dining room, pulled out the chair for me to sit down, and then sat down across from me where the food cart was...

"Oh my God – there's so much food!"

"We've worked up enough of an appetite to handle it..." Bazil said as he put all the food on the table...

"Are you going to talk to our son the way your father talked to you?" I asked as we started eating the Antipasto Assorted Cheese, Charcuterie Meats..."

"Absolutely..."

"What if we have a girl – will you talk to her too?" I asked as I we put some Artisanal Cheeses with Seasonal Accompaniments on our plate and continued eating...

"Absolutely – I'll probably talk to her more..." he answered as the put the Tuxedo Strawberries on our plate...

"Me too - those look good..."

"I agree..." he agreed as we continued eating...

"Will you talk to our son?" he asked as he put the Double Chocolate Brownies and Blondie Cake Pops on our plate...

"Of course!"

"Just checking..." he laughed...

"Oh my God – these are sooo good!" I said as I tasted the brownies...

"You're right – they are good..." he agreed...

"I'm not sure what I'll say to our daughter though..."

"Why not?"

"I can talk to her – but how do I tell our daughter to make sure the dick is good?"

"You tell her the same thing I'm going to tell her..."

"What are you going to tell her?"

"I'm going to tell her to make sure she has a man that listens..." he answered as he started eating the blondie cake pop..."

"Aww... I love you..." I said as I put the blondie cake pop in my mouth...

"I love you too..."

"Have you always wanted children?" I asked as I picked up the Sin City Angus Burger and took a bite...

"Yes..." he answered as he picked up his burger and took a bite...

"Me too..." I said as I finished my burger and started my fries. We continued eating until we were finished and then Bazil spoke...

"Come with me..." he said as I stood up and he led me over to the Chaise Lounge in front of the window... "Lay down..." he commanded. I did as I was told and watched him go to the bar and make an Amaretto Sour. Bazil came back over to the lounger, sat down beside me, and passed me the glass... "Drink..." I took a sip; Bazil kissed me, and sucked the Amaretto off my tongue... "Mmmm..." he moaned. Bazil took a sip and kissed me again, this time allowing me to suck the Amaretto off his tongue...

"Mmmm..." I moaned. We continued taking turns, sipping, drinking, and sucking each other's tongues, until the glass was empty...

"You like cumming with my dick in your mouth... don't you?"

"Yesss..."

"I can tell when you're ready to cum... you start sucking my dick harder..."

"You like that?"

"Hell Yea!" he breathed... "What makes you wanna suck my dick?"

"I love making you feel good..."

"Aww... I love you..."

"I love it when you grab my head play in my hair, and talk dirty when I suck it..."

"Oh yea?"

"Yea..."

"I love tasting you..."

"You do?"

"Hell yea – you taste good, you get wet, and you quench my thirst..."

"I taste good?"

"Hell yea..."

"Aww... thank you..."

"You're welcome…"

"It feels so good…" I breathed…

"You're imagining me sucking your pussy right now… aren't you?"

"Yeesss…."

"Close your eyes…"

"Okay…" I breathed…

"Slide down in the chair a little…"

"Okay…"

"Spread your legs…"

"Okay…

"Keep your eyes closed… and imagine me sucking on your pussy…"

"Huh… Bazil…"

"Touch yourself…"

"Bazil…" I moaned as I started rubbing my clit…"

"Keep your eyes closed… and imagine my tongue going up and down…"

"Ohhh…. Ooohhh…"

"Imagine my tongue fucking your pussy…"

"Bazil… Huh… Fuck…" Bazil got up, came up towards my face, and startled me by putting his dick in my mouth…

"Keep your eyes closed…"

"Mmmm…. Mmmm…." I moaned as he fucked my mouth slowly…

"Imagine me sucking your clit while you're sucking my dick…" he whispered as he grabbed my head and pushed his dick in my mouth further…

"Hmmmm.... Hmmmm.... Hmmm...." I moaned on his dick as I started cumming...

"Yes... that's it... imagine yourself cumming... in my mouth... as I'm cumming... in yours!" he growled as we both came simultaneously...

"MMMMM... MMMMM... MMMMM... MMMMM... MMMMM!"

"UUUGH! UUUGH! UUUGH! UUUGH! UUUGH! How'd that feel?" he asked as I took his dick out my mouth, opened my eyes, and looked up at him...

"Fuck me..." I breathed...

"Is that what you want?" he asked as he looked down at me...

"Yes... my Thirst Quencher..." I breathed as I stood up...

"Come with me..." he said as he took me by the hand, led me to the bed, pushed me down onto the bed, climbed on top of me, eased himself inside me, put his tongue in my mouth, covered my mouth with his, and fucked me for the rest of the night.

# Chapter 6

I was in complete awe as we walked into Osgood Publishing. "Welcome back Mr. Osgood," someone greeted.

"Sam – how many times do I have to tell you..."

"Welcome back Bazil," Sam said as he grabbed Bazil into a hug.

"This is my wife, Beautiee..." Bazil said as he introduced me.

"Wife? What? – I mean – hell – congratulations!" Sam said as he grabbed me into a hug...

"Thanks..." I laughed.

"Oh – my bad – I'm sorry..." he laughed as he let me go...

"Honey... who's this?" she asked playfully as she walked up towards me...

"I'm Bazil's wife, Beautiee..." I smiled.

"Wife? What?" she said as she grabbed me into a hug...

"Ummm... thank you... who are you?" I laughed.

"Oh... I'm sorry.... I'm Joselyn, Sam's wife, Sam's assistant, and Bazil's 2nd assistant," she laughed as she let me go...

"I guess I got my answer..." I laughed.

"Umm... what was the question?" another lady laughed as she walked up to me...

"Well – I was nervous about meeting you all but I can see I had nothing to worry about," I answered.

"Well who are you?" the lady laughed.

"Mother – that's Bazil's new wife, Beautiee," Joselyn answered.

"Oh my God – congratulations – Bazil – you didn't tell me you were seeing anyone!" she laughed as she hugged me...

"I wasn't aware I had to..." Bazil laughed.

"And who are you?" I asked as everyone got quiet...

"Well... since you asked... I'm Sheila. I'm the Chief Financial Officer. This is the Vice President, my son-in-law, Samuel, and this is his wife, my daughter, Joselyn."

"Well it's lovely to meet you Sheila," I said. Bazil stood to the side beaming with pride and I continued with Sheila as I observed another woman walking up on the conversation... "Bazil and I met a little over a week ago...

"A week ago?"

"Yea..."

"Oh I need to hear this... Bazil, we'll be back – we're going for coffee – come with me

Beautiee – you too Joselyn – oh hi MaryJane – this is Beautiee, Bazil's wife – we're going for coffee – you wanna join us?"

"No thank you – nice meeting you though..." she said as she turned to walk towards Bazil and Sam...

"We'll stop in the cafeteria – they make good coffee here," Sheila said as I followed them through the glass doors...

"How do you like your coffee?" Joselyn asked as I sat at one of the tables...

"Hazelnut flavor, hazelnut creamer, light and sweet," I answered.

"Just how Bazil likes 'em..." Sheila laughed as Joselyn walked off to get us coffee... "So tell me how this happened..." Sheila said.

"Well, I met Bazil about a week ago at the Hotel Zero Degrees in Stamford. I was having a drink, he came up to get a drink, we started talking, we hit it off..."

"Hit it off?" Sheila asked...

"Yea..." I answered as I started drifting off...

"Here's your coffee Beautiee," Joselyn said as she sat down with us.

"Beautiee was telling me she met Bazil at the Hotel Zero Degrees a week ago," Sheila said as we started drinking our coffee...

"It happens Ma – you know me and Sam..."

"Yes Joselyn – I know, I know," Sheila laughed.

"Well I don't know – tell me," I laughed.

"I knew I was gonna marry Sam the moment I met him – I didn't know when – but I knew it..." Joselyn answered.

"I had no idea I was getting married – I still can't believe he asked me that night..." I sighed...

"That night? At the hotel?" Sheila asked...

"Well... technically... it wasn't until the next day... before checkout..." I sighed...

"Oh wow..." Joselyn sighed...

"So he met you at the bar... y'all spent the night together... and he proposed the next morning?" Sheila asked...

"Well... technically it was the afternoon... we had a late check out..." I sighed as I drifted off again...

"Well I like you already – you have a nice spirit," Sheila said.

"Awww... thank you..." I said with tears in my eyes...

"You're welcome – so are you going to be working here with Bazil?" she asked.

"Yes I am..." I answered.

"Oh boy – does MaryJane know that?" Joselyn asked.

"I'm sure she does now..." Sheila answered... "And if the doesn't, she goin' learn taday!" she laughed.

"Who's MaryJane?" I asked...

"She's the one who I invited to come get coffee – I knew she wasn't coming anyway – with her stank ass!" Sheila laughed.

"Ma!" Joselyn exclaimed.

"Please Joselyn – you could do her job better – she walks around here like she owns the place... and Bazil..." Sheila said as we continued to sip on our coffee...

"Oh I forgot – I need to get them stats done – le'me run to the bathroom right quick before I miss the deadline," Joselyn said as she darted out of the cafeteria...

"I might as well go to the bathroom – you can make that the 2nd room on the office tour," I laughed.

"Okay – follow me..." Sheila said as she got up and I followed her to the bathroom...

"Oh my God – why?" I heard Joselyn ask...

"She may be nice... for now... until she gets comfortable... then she'll start thinking she runs shit... and I'll have to check her... just like I had to check Janet," I heard MaryJane say. Sheila and I looked at each other and then we both looked back towards the bathroom door...

"You ain't right MaryJane..." Joselyn said.

"Please Joselyn... I've been here for too long to let a Bitch come up in here and knock me outta my position..."

"What position? Your job?"

"That's only part of it..."

"What else is there?"

"She won't last... she may be his wife... for now..."

"What's that supposed to mean?"

"It's only temporary Joselyn," MaryJane answered as she snatched the bathroom door open to exit... and ran right into me...

"Hello MaryJane," I said deliberately as she tried to pass me without excusing herself...

"Oh... Hello Beautiee..." she said...

"Mrs. Osgood," I said, correcting her.

"Excuse me?" MaryJane snapped...

"Please call me Mrs. Osgood," I said as I walked past her, went into the stall, and closed the door. When I came out the stall and went to wash my hands, Sheila spoke...

"Are you okay Beautiee – I mean Mrs. Osgood?"

"Yea... I made it without incident," I answered purposely changing the subject as I washed my hands...

"Ummmmm... I'ma go now..." Joselyn said as she left the bathroom and Sheila followed behind her. I stood there taking my time drying my hands as they spoke on the other side of the door... "Ma... did she hear what MaryJane said?"

"We both did," Sheila answered. I opened the door and walked out into the hallway...

"Sheila, could you please escort me back to my husband's office?"

"Yes Mrs. Osgood — I'll see you later Joselyn," she said as we walked away. I was seething and Sheila knew it, but she didn't say anything as we walked towards Bazil's office.

# Chapter 7

"So… you married now huh?"

"Yes I am."

"Does she know about Janet?"

"That's nothing for you to be concerned with…"

"What about me?"

"You'll be fine… as long as you continue to behave…"

"I need to get back to my desk… I'll see you later…" Sheila whispered as she walked away and I continued to listen…

"Who the fuck do you think you're talking to muthafucka?" MaryJane snapped…

"Who the fuck do you think you're talking to?" Bazil growled as he grabbed her throat…

"Bazil… I'm sorry… I can't breathe…"

"You ever speak to me like that again and you won't ever breathe again… are we clear?"

"As clear as we were when you had your dick in my mouth…" she said as she sat down on the sofa and started to unfasten his belt…

"Beautiee... I.... I didn't hear you come in..." Bazil stuttered as I stormed over to the couch, grabbed MaryJane by the back of her hair, and dragged her across the floor towards the door...

"You got 10 seconds to get your ass up and get the fuck off the premises – and let me make myself clear – if I catch your ass back on the premises or anywhere near my husband again – I'll blow your fuckin' head off!" Bazil stood there with his mouth open as Sheila, Sam, Joselyn, and a few other employees watched MaryJane run to her desk, grab her pocket book and keys, and fly out the door... "Joselyn – I need you to clean out your desk!" I said as I walked towards Bazil's office and pushed him inside...

"I'm getting fired? Why?" Joselyn asked as she started to cry...

"Joselyn – I said I need you to clean out your desk!" I repeated as I went into Bazil's office and slammed the door...

"Beautiee... I'm sorry..."

"You fuckin' that Bitch?"

"I was..."

"Who is it?" I snapped...

"Joselyn..."

"Come in Joselyn..." I said as I looked at Bazil and Joselyn came inside, sat on the sofa, and put a box of personal items on the floor... "Joselyn – since MaryJane no longer works here – we need a personal assistant – I'm offering the position to you... if you're interested..." I said as I sat down beside her and took her hand...

"Thank you Mrs. Osgood..." she breathed as she sighed with relief...

"You're welcome – I'll need you to start immediately – that's why I asked you to clean out your desk...

"Oooohhh... okay...."

"Since you'll be working for both of us you're going to have additional responsibilities... so we'll make your raise retro-active starting today – Bazil, can you take care of the paperwork so I can get settle in?"

"Yes Beautiee," Bazil answered as he went out into the hall...

"Bazil – is my wife getting fired?" Sam asked.

"No Sam – but she won't be working for you any longer..."

"What happened Bazil?"

"My wife fired MaryJane... and promoted your wife..." Bazil answered as he smiled...

"Oh shit!"

"I'm on my way to get her paperwork started – my wife instructed me to make her raise effective today..."

"I love your wife!" Sam exclaimed...

"I love her too..." Bazil said...

"So MaryJane is gone for good?"

"I'm surprised you didn't hear about it..."

"Hear about what?"

"Your wife didn't tell you?"

"My wife was too upset..."

"Well... MaryJane forgot her place... she spoke outta turn... and my wife heard what she said..."

"Oh shit! What the fuck happened?"

"My wife snatched the Bitch by her hair... dragged her across the floor... and told her she had 10 seconds to get the fuck off the premises!" Bazil laughed...

"What?! And I missed it?!"

"You missed it..."

"Bazil... you're not worried?"

"Fuck her..." Bazil laughed...

"Damn Bazil... that's fucked up..."

"She fucked up..."

"Bazil... she could file a lawsuit for wrongful termination..."

"And she could also be permanently terminated..." Bazil said as Joselyn and I came out into the hallway...

"Hey Sam – did Bazil tell you the news?" I asked as I walked past them with Joselyn...

"Yes he did – congratulations baby," Sam said as he pulled his wife into a kiss, causing her to drop the box... "Sorry baby – le'me get that for you – where are we going?"

"We're going to your wife's new office," I answered.

"Yes Maam," Sam said as he walked towards MaryJane's old office...

"Mrs. Osgood," I corrected."

"Yes Mrs. Osgood," Sam acknowledged as Bazil headed over to payroll and I walked to Joselyn's new office with Sam...

"Oh my God – is everything okay?" Sheila yelled as she came running into the office...

"Yes Mother," Joselyn answered.

"Isn't this MaryJane's office?" Sheila asked...

"She no longer works here," I answered...

"Ooookkkaaayyyy...." Sheila said as she backed out of the office...

"Joselyn – please come see me as soon as you get settled – Sam – I need you to call a staff meeting asap!"

"Yes Mrs. Osgood," Sam said as he hurried down the hall to get Bazil...

"Joselyn – where do they hold staff meetings at?"

"They usually hold them in conference room 1," she answered as she continued unpacking her box and setting up her new desk..."

"Thank you Joselyn," I said as I hurried to the conference room...

"Hey Beautiee..." Bazil said nervously as I walked over to him... "Are you getting settled in okay?"

"Thank you all for coming," I said as Sheila, Joselyn, and other employees came into the conference room. "Sam, could you close the door please?"

"Yes Mrs. Osgood," Sam said as he went to the door and closed it...

"For those of you who don't know me, I'm Mrs. Osgood." I watched for a moment as some of the employees started whispering... "I know you're all shocked... I'm still in shock myself," I said as I wrapped my arm around Bazil and stood beside him. "I'll be working alongside my husband and I will also be making personnel changes as I deem necessary," I continued. I watched again as some of the employees started whispering... "Having said that, I have two announcements," I continued... "First - effective immediately — MaryJane LaRue no longer works here – furthermore, she is not to be near or on the premises..." I watched again as some of the employees whispered and others gasped... "Second – effective immediately – Joselyn Logan has been promoted to our Personal Assistant." I watched, listened, and observed as all the employees got up to congratulate Joselyn...

"My baby!" Sheila yelled...

"'Bout damn time..."

"Girl – I'm so happy for you..."

"Yes Honey!"

"Congratulations!"

"Thank you, thank you, thank you..." Joselyn said in between hugs. I watched as the employees went to sit back down...

"So let me tell you a little bit about myself. I've always been a writer. Growing up in foster care comes with a great deal of challenges, and writing was how I dealt with them." I watched and observed as everyone got eerily quiet, eager to hear what I had to say – and it made me smile. "As a child, I would write songs, poems, and essays. When it was time for me to graduate from elementary school, the Principal asked us to write an essay about our experiences and I wrote an essay about the way they teased me when I had eye surgery and had to wear prisms on my glasses – I even wrote a song about it to help me cope." Some of the employees looked at each other nodding and shaking their heads as I continued... "I was surprised when the principal told me my essay was chosen to be read at the Graduation Assembly and I sang the song I wrote to the Assembly. I continued writing through high school and college – partly because it was required – but mostly because I really enjoyed it and still do. Along with writing, I was also reading - in fact, I read so much my grandmother used to yell at me when I went grocery shopping with her because I'd always read the labels on the canned foods and desserts before I put them in the cart." Everyone burst into laughter. I waited for them all to calm down before I continued. "As

I got older, I would read books, critique them, and change the ending by saying 'I would have said this, I would have done that. My friends would always tell me you should write a book and I would always say one day – and one day finally came. I published my 1st book with a vanity publisher in 2003, I made mistakes, and I learned what I didn't like about vanity publishers. Since writing is in my blood, rather than give up on publishing, I went to writing expos, author signings, etc., and learned some more. The turning point for me was when I had a one-on-one with Michael Baisden who sat with me, gave me advice, and took out his tape recorder to make a note when he thought I had a good idea. I turned my first book into a 5-book series, and I was ready to publish them but I knew I wasn't going back to vanity publishing so I reached out to David L. at Total Package Publications. He referred me to selfpublishing.com, and they gave me step-by-step instructions on the entire process from purchasing your own ISBN numbers to starting your own publishing company, so I started Beautiful Publications in 2014 and published my series myself." Bazil was so proud standing there. The room was quiet until Joselyn raised her hand… "Yes Joselyn?"

"Where can we buy your books?"

"You can't."

"Why not?"

"Because you work for me so I won't sell them to you – but what I will do is give you all copies for your review if you'd like..."

"Oooohhhh..." all the employees said in unison.

"Now that you know a lil' something about me I'm looking forward to getting to know a lil' something about you too – in time – right now though, I need to get settled and get up to speed – Joselyn – I need you to clear my husband's calendar for the rest of the day – Sam I need you to handle whatever comes up – we'll see everyone tomorrow..." I said as I took Bazil by the hand and we went to his office...

"Come here Beautiee..." Bazil said as he pulled me into a kiss... "I'm so proud of how you took charge and handled business today..." Bazil said as I tried to pull away from him..." Beautiee... please... I didn't mean for that to happen..."

"I know... let go of me..."

"Is that what you want?"

"Yes Bazil..."

"Okay... if that's what you want..." he said as he let me go and sat down on the sofa...

"How many times did you fuck her on this couch Bazil?"

"Beautiee... please..."

"Answer me Bazil..."

"A few months..." Bazil whispered as he put his head in his hands...

"I was so happy when I got up this morning – I couldn't wait to come here – I was so happy that everyone started to like me..." I said as I started crying...

"Beautiee... please don't cry... I'm sorry..."

"Let me finish Bazil..."

"Okay..." he said with tears in his eyes...

"Sheila took me to the cafeteria with Joselyn and we had coffee – I was telling them how we met and you proposed the next day..." I said as I began to smile. Bazil started to smile before I continued... "Joselyn was telling me how she knew she was going to marry Sam the moment she met him..."

"Aww... that's beautiful... he loves her as much as I love you..."

"That isn't possible," I laughed.

"You're right," Bazil laughed...

"Anyway... Joselyn said she had to finish her stats so she went to the ladies room... Sheila and I finished our coffee and I said we might as well go too – I even joked about her making it part of the office tour..."

"Sounds like you hit it off..."

"That's exactly what I told her about me and you," I said as I smiled. Bazil took my hand as I continued... "Sheila told me in the cafeteria that MaryJane walked around like she owned the place... and you..."

"Sheila never liked MaryJane..."

"After what we heard I understand why she didn't like her..."

"What?" Bazil interrupted...

"When we got to the ladies room we heard MaryJane talking to Joselyn... about me..."

"Oh hell no..." Bazil whispered...

"She told Joselyn that she worked here too long to let a Bitch knock her out of her position..."

"And Sheila heard this conversation?"

"We both did..."

"Did she say anything else?"

"She told Joselyn as soon as I got comfortable she was going to have to check me... like she had to check Janet... who's Janet Bazil?" Bazil didn't answer me right away. His eyes turned to slits and the vein in his neck started twitching. His blood was boiling and I could feel the anger coming from him...

"Janet was my first wife - but what else did she say?"

"I'm afraid to tell you Bazil..."

"Beautiee please... I'm not going to hurt you..."

"I know you won't hurt me... but you might hurt her..."

"Beautiee... what... did... she... say?"

"She said I may be your wife for now... but it's only temporary..."

"And Sheila heard this entire conversation?"

"Yes."

"I need to speak to Sheila immediately," Bazil said as he went to get up...

"You need to speak to me right now Bazil..."

"You're right... I'm sorry..."

"Sheila walked me back to your office... and she heard some of what MaryJane said to you before she walked away..."

"Oh God – please tell me she didn't hear that Bitch say she had my dick in her mouth..." Bazil moaned...

"She didn't hear that – but I did – remember?"

"I'm sorry... I wish I never met that Bitch – she better be glad it was you that dragged her ass outta here and not me..."

"You would've been in jail Bazil..."

"I've been there before..."

"Where would that leave me Bazil?"

"You're right... I'm sorry..."

"Everything was going so good until that Bitch forgot her place – and I had to put her back in it..."

"I'm so sorry..."

"When I heard her say she had your dick in her mouth I lost it - I could've killed her - I meant what I said Bazil - if I catch her anywhere near you again... I'll make good on that promise..."

"I know..."

"You know?"

"I saw how you took care of business... and so did everyone else..."

"I'm not proud of that Bazil – that's not how my first day was supposed to be..."

"Yes it was..."

"Bazil!"

"Beautiee... listen to me..." Bazil said as he took my face in his hands and kissed me... "Trust me... after what I witnessed today in your first meeting as my wife, my business partner – you have their admiration – and you have their respect..." he said as he continued to kiss me...

"Bazil..." I interrupted...

"Yes Beautiee..." he breathed as he kissed me again...

"What happened to Janet?" Bazil let go of me and stared out the window for a few moments before he answered me...

"She died." I didn't ask any more questions. I got up, left Bazil sitting on the sofa, and went to Joselyn's office...

"Joselyn – please come with me," I said as I waited for her to get up...

"Yes Mrs. Osgood," she said as she followed me back to Bazil's office...

"Close the door Joselyn," I said as Bazil looked back and forth between the two of us...

"Is something wrong Mrs. Osgood?" Joselyn asked.

"Something's definitely wrong Joselyn – I need you to get me an interior designer – I want this office done from top to bottom – I want new lighting – I want calm soothing colors – and I also want this wall gone so my desk will fit in here along with my husband's – I want his name on this door and my name on the other door – are you getting this Joselyn?"

"I gotchu you – go 'head," she laughed.

"You wanna add anything Bazil?" I asked.

"As long as I don't walk into a women's lounge you can do whatever you want," Bazil laughed.

"Don't worry Bazil – oh – before I forget – Joselyn?"

"Yes Mrs. Osgood?"

"This fuckin' couch has got to go – tonight!"

"Yes Mrs. Osgood – Sam · I need your help!" she yelled out to her husband as Bazil and I left.

# Chapter 8

"Excuse me – Mrs. Osgood?"

"Yes Joselyn?"

"I need y'all to come with me..."

"Is everything okay?" Bazil asked...

"I need y'all to come with me..." Joselyn repeated...

"Okay... we're coming..." I said as we followed Joselyn to the lobby...

"Surprise!" everyone yelled...

"Oh my God, oh my God, oh my God!" I screamed as I jumped up and down and ran to hug David Bromstad from HGTV...

"I guess you know who I am..." David laughed as he hugged me back...

"Bazil... did you know about this?" I asked...

"I had no idea – I'm Bazil Osgood," Bazil said as he extended his hand to shake David's hand...

"I'm David Bromstad from Colorspash on HGTV," David beamed as he shook Bazil's hand and the cameras filmed us live...

"Oooohhh look... its David Bromstad!" a few of the employees shouted as they came running towards the lobby...

"We're here today because we received a letter from one of your employees..." David said as Bazil and I started looking around... "Is there a Joselyn Logan here?" David asked...

"I'm Joselyn!" Joselyn beamed as she went towards David and gave him a hug...

"Joselyn wrote us a letter explaining that you were looking to have your office re-decorated and that you specifically wanted light, bright and airy colors," David beamed as he wrapped his arm around Joselyn before continuing... "Joselyn also told us you're newlyweds," David said...

"Yes we are..." Bazil answered, pulling me close to him...

"I love love, romance, and weddings – so when we received this letter from Joselyn – I told the producers we have to do this and the producers agreed – it's our wedding gift to you," David beamed.

"Oh my Goooddddd!" I screamed as I jumped up and down... "Thank you, thank you, thank you!"

"You're welcome – we need to wrap this up so what I'd like to do is go to your office, discuss options, and show you what I've come up with..." David said as the crew members came closer...

"Our office is down the hall here..." Bazil said as we went down the hall to the office. Once we got inside David began to do what he does best...

"I understand you want to expand and you want this wall down – is that correct?"

"Yes it is," I beamed.

"Mr. Osgood – is there anything that's off limits?" David asked...

"As long as I'm not walking into a women's lounge, I'm fine..." Bazil laughed...

"I understand – now I have a few ideas I'd like to show you..." David said as he took out his drawings...

"Oh wow – these are nice!" Bazil said as he looked at them... "Beautiee – what do you think?" he asked as he handed the drawings to me...

"I like them all... but this one stands out..." I said pointing to the $3^{rd}$ drawing...

"I was hoping you'd pick that one – it's actually my favorite..." David gushed...

"We'll go with that one then..." Bazil said as he pulled me close to him...

"I can't wait to get started – we'll get that wall down first thing – once we do that, your new office will be done in about a week..." David said.

"That soon?" Bazil asked...

"Oh yea – by the way – is there another office you can use in the meantime?" David asked...

"You can use my office..." Joselyn volunteered...

"Thank you Joselyn – but where will you go?" I asked...

"I'll go in the office with my husband until your office is ready..." Joselyn answered.

"Thank you Joselyn..." I said as I hugged her...

"You're welcome Mrs. Osgood..."

"Hey everyone – what's going on?" Sam asked as he walked in...

"We're going to be on HGTV..." Bazil answered...

"Oh wow – how'd that happen?"

"Your wife wrote them a letter and told them we were newlyweds, so David Bromstad is designing our new office as a wedding gift to us..."

"Babe... you did?" Sam asked...

"I did..." Joselyn beamed...

"How'd I get such an awesome wife?" Sam asked as he pulled Joselyn into a kiss..."

"You prayed for me..." Joselyn answered as the cameras continued filming...

# Chapter 9

"I can't believe I went all the way over there just to find out they canceled my appointment..." I sighed as I pulled into the driveway. "Hmmmmm... I see Trevor's car – he must have stopped by to see Bazil..." I said as I got out. I walked up to the door, knocked, and waited... "Hmmmmm... they must be in the library..." I said as I started digging in my pocket book for my keys... "Got em!" I said out loud as I opened the door and let myself in... "Bazil – can you believe I went all the way over there just to find out they cancelled my appointment? Bazil? Baby where are you? Oh – I know – in the library getting your drink on huh..." I said as I went towards the library...

"BAZZZZIIILLL!!! OH MY GODDDD!!!! WHAT THE FUCK ARE YOU DOING????!!!!"

"Beautiee... I can explain..." Bazil said as he jumped up off of Trevor. I grabbed the bottle of scotch and threw it across the library towards the couch where Trevor was scrambling to pull up his pants. The glass broke and broken glass mixed with scotch hit the back of the couch and dripped onto the bottom of the couch and onto the floor. I looked back toward Bazil and I saw him standing there with a condom on his dick.... And I went ballistic... Bazil's eyes got really big as I grabbed a bottle of Hennessey and threw it towards Trevor – and this time I didn't miss...

"Aaaahhh!" Trevor cried out as the bottle hit him in his head. I started laughing maniacally when I saw the gash over Trevor's eye with blood gushing out. Bazil charged towards me as I grabbed the letter opener...

"I'LL KILL YOU!!!" I screamed as I lunged at Bazil with the letter opener but Bazil jumped out of the way so I ended up stabbing the door instead...

"Beautiee... Baby... please... put that down... you're going to hurt yourself..." Bazil said as Trevor jumped up from the couch and ran out while Bazil had my attention diverted...

"You're right..." I said calmly... "I should put this down... and you should clean this mess up... I'm going out... I'll be back later..." I said as I picked up my keys, put my pocket book on my shoulder, and went to sit in the car... "Mutha Fuckin' best friend my ass – NO! – His ass!" I said as I started laughing maniacally, put the car in drive, and drove straight to the Holiday Inn Express. "I need a room please!" I snapped when I got to the counter...

"Do you have a reservation maam?"

"No..." I sighed...

"Let me see if we have anything available... hmmmmm... I'm sorry... we're booked solid..."

"Please... I really need a room... I'll take anything..." I pleaded as my eyes filled with tears..."

"Well... we have a King Leisure Suite available... if they don't check in..."

"What time is check-in?"

"Check-in starts at 4pm and ends at 9pm... unless you call to ask us to extend it... then it can go up to midnight..."

"Did you get a call to request a late check-in?"

"Nope... and it will be 9pm in 5... 4... 3...2...1 – now we just wait for the room to be released and... okay – I can check you in right now!" She smiled...

"Thank you soooo much... I really appreciate it..." I breathed as I gave her my Black Card...

"Mrs. Osgood! Oh my goodness – why didn't you say so! It's so nice to finally meet you in person! I'm Shireen!" she said as she came from behind the counter to give me a hug...

"Nice to meet you Shireen..." I said as I hugged her back... "So you know my husband?"

"Yes I do... he comes here with Trevor whenever they have business..."

"Is that right?" I asked as my blood began to boil...

"Yea – they come here for drinks too – Trevor is fine – if I wasn't already married he could definitely git it – oh my God – I can't believe I just said that – excuse me!"

"Oh that's okay Shireen – we can keep it between us girls..." I laughed as I took my card and my key...

"Have a good night – nice meeting you!" she yelled as I went towards the elevator...

"Mutha fucka been fuckin' Trevor here huh – thanks for telling me Shireen!" I gritted as I punched the button for my floor. When the doors opened, I got off the elevator and saw my room was to the right... "Good – easy to find..." I said as I opened the door and went into the room... "I need a drink..." I said as I went straight to the bar. My cell phone started ringing so I picked it up and saw it was Bazil... "Fuck You Mutha Fucka!" I yelled as I threw the phone on the bed and poured myself a glass of Jack Daniels... "Aaahhh yess... just what I needed..." I said as I gulped it down. I sat on the bed, picked up my cell phone, and called Trevor...

"Baby... is that you?" he answered...

"It's me Baby..." I answered eerily...

"Beautiee... how'd you get this number?"

"Meet me at the Holiday Inn Express..."

"Hell no Bitch – you just tried to take my fuckin' head off – are you crazy?"

"You fucked my husband – I tried to take your fuckin' head off – one good fuck deserves another... and I'm on a mission to collect..."

"Wait... What?"

"I want you to fuck me Trevor..."

"Are you serious?"

"I'm in room 432..." I answered... and then hung up. I poured myself another drink, gulped it down, lay down on the bed, and fell asleep...

"Mmmm.... Bazil... somebody's at the door..." I yawned as I stretched... "Shit – I forgot where the hell I was for a sec..." I said as I got up to answer the door. "Come in Trevor..." I said as I opened the door. Trevor came into the room, closed the door behind him, and walked towards the bar...

"Mind if I pour myself a drink?"

"Help yourself – and pour me another one while you're at it..." I said as I walked over to the bar, took the glass from him, and gulped it down...

"Thirsty huh?" Trever asked as he sipped his drink...

"Finish your drink Trevor..." I demanded as I pulled back the blankets and sheets, sat on the bed, and started undressing myself. Trevor did as he was told, stood up, and started to undress...

I got up out the bed and went to the bathroom. When I came out the bathroom I threw a red towel at him...

"Come back to bed... we have the rest of the night..." he said as he started wiping his crotch...

"No thank you... thanks though..." I said.

"Oh... it's like that?"

"Like what?"

"So... you're finished?"

"Basically..."

"Oh that's fucked up..."

"Ya know – it's a shame you're not straight," I said as I put my put my bag on my shoulder. "You're nice lookin', you have a good job, a nice portfolio – you could use a refresher course in how to please a woman but overall, I'd say you have potential," I said as I put on my coat and headed towards the door...

"Fuck you Bitch!" he yelled.

"You just did – thanks!" I said as I slammed the door and headed down the corridor towards the elevator.

# Chapter 10

"Well, well, well... look who finally decided to come home," Bazil said as I came in.

"Home? Yea right," I laughed.

"Do you have any idea what time it is?" he asked.

"Is the clock broke?" I answered.

"Don't play with me Beautiee!" he snapped.

"I wasn't planning to," I said.

"Oh you got jokes? Okay..." he said as he got up off the couch and followed me into the kitchen...

"Where's the wine?" I asked as I looked in the cabinets.

"You think you can do whatever-the-fuck you want right?" he asked as he came up behind me and grabbed me by the back of the neck...

"I know I can – now get the fuck off me!" I yelled as I elbowed him in the ribs. When he let go of me to recover from wincing in pain, I slid from between him and the counter and started to run out the kitchen, but he caught me by my hair...

"Get your ass back here Beautiee!" he growled as he yanked me back in the kitchen and threw me into the edge of the granite counter top. When he saw the tears in my eyes he laughed. "I'm gonna make you regret the day you ever met me," he said as he pinned me against the counter with his body, bracing himself against the counter with his right hand.

"I've regretted the day I met you ever since I found out you've been fucking Trevor!" I snapped as I pushed him away from me. He didn't say anything. He just stood there, staring through me as I watched his nostrils flare.

"You had no business fucking him," he breathed as he came towards me again, gritting his teeth.

"You wanna die?" I asked as I grabbed the knife...

"You don't have it in you," he said as he got closer... close enough for me to stab him in his hand...

"Guess again!" I yelled as I plunged the knife into the palm of his left hand on the counter...

"I'll kill you!" he growled as he grabbed the knife out of the palm of his hand and headed towards me with it...

"Is everything alright?" Keisha asked as she knocked on the door.

"Thank you Lord," I said as I opened the door... "Hey Keisha..." I said with my head down.

"Girl, what's wrong?" she asked as she pushed her way into the living room and sat down on the couch. "You're bleeding Bazil – oh my God – what happened?"

"She stabbed me," Bazil answered.

"What?! Is that true Beautiee?"

"Sure is!"

"Call the police Keisha..." Bazil said.

"Somebody already did – it sounded like a gun went off in here."

"Who is it?" I snapped as I heard knocking...

"Police..." she said. Bazil stood there giving me the evil eye as I walked towards the door.

"May I help you?" I asked.

"My name is Detective Jones... may I come in?"

"Sure," I said as I opened the door and let her in...

"Hi, I'm Detective Jones... but my friends call me Katina," she said as she extended her hand..."

"I'm Beautiee... and this is my husband Bazil," I said as I pointed over to Bazil...

"We know each other," Bazil said, not moving from where he was standing...

"May I sit?" Katina asked.

"Sure," I said as I sat with her on the couch...

"I'll get you ladies something to drink," Bazil said as he headed towards the kitchen...

"Are you okay?" Katina whispered.

"Yea... I'm just pissed off," I sighed.

"Your neighbor said you were fighting..."

"Yea... we were..."

"I don't see any bruises... did he hurt you?"

"It wasn't that kinda fight," I laughed "We just cursed each other out..."

"Your neighbor said she heard gun shots..."

"I bet she did... we were watching Law and Order..."

"Okay... that makes sense..."

"Ladies," Bazil said as he handed us our drinks... "I gave you ginger ale Katina... I hope that's alright..." Bazil said as I sipped and observed...

"Oh that's fine – I'm on duty," she said as she finished her ginger ale...

"Well... don't let us keep you," Bazil said as he directed her towards the front door...

"Alrighty then," she laughed as she went to leave...

"Bazil?"

"Yes Beautiee?"

"Could you make me another drink while I see Katina out?"

"Sure," Bazil answered as he looked at me perplexed before going back into the kitchen...

"Thanks for stopping by," I said as I opened the door for her to leave...

"Be careful Beautiee," she whispered as she handed me her card... "Your husband's a dangerous man," she whispered again as I closed the door behind her...

"What was that all about?" Bazil asked as he handed me a drink and walked me back towards the living room...

"You..."

"What'd she say?"

"She said I need to be careful because you're dangerous," I answered as I finished my drink...

"I'll be back later Beautiee," Bazil said as he put on his jacket and picked up his keys...

"Bazil?"

"Yes Beautiee?"

"Did you fuck her?"

"Hell no!" he said as he went out, closing the door behind him.

# Chapter 11

"Beautiee... I'm home," Bazil yelled as he came inside, hung up his jacket, and went into the living room... "Beautiee... where are you?" Bazil called as he went into the kitchen and found my letter on the counter...

"Hey my Thirst Quencher," Bazil read as he picked up the letter... "I'm sorry I hurt you. I love you so much and if I had to marry you all over again, I would. When I married you, I promised you I'd love you forever... and I will... but I can't get that image of you and Trevor out of my head. I thought I'd feel better after having sex with Trevor but to be honest, I feel like shit. I had sex with Trevor to hurt you because when I saw you with him it broke my heart – because I know you love him too – and I don't know if I can share you or your heart with anyone else. When you asked me to marry you, you promised me you'd make me feel good every day for the rest of my life – and you broke that promise."

"Beautiee... I'm so sorry..." Bazil said out loud as he broke down crying...

"I'm back home. Please give me time. I'll call you when I'm ready. Love, Beautiee."

"This can't be happening..." Bazil cried as he picked up the phone to call Trevor...
"Hey Baby," Trevor answered...
"She's gone," Bazil whispered.
"She left you?"
"She left me Trevor," he said as he broke down crying again...
"I'm sorry Baby... you want me to come over?"
"That's what got me into this shit in the first place..."
"You're right Baby... I'm sorry... you wanna come back here?"
"No Trevor... I'll call you later..."

"Damn... I never thought I'd be back here," I said out loud as I closed the door and locked it. "Let me check my phone..."
"You have no new messages."
"Good thing I didn't turn off the cable... I need a dose of reality TV," I said out loud as I plopped down on the couch... "Let's see... Monday night... Hmmmmm... Love & Hip Hop should be on," I said out loud as I turned on the TV. After flicking through the channels, I got

bored, and went into the kitchen... "Where's my wine... Ohhh... Thank God," I said out loud as I poured myself a glass of wine, picked up the bottle, and sat back down on the couch. I started drinking from the glass and picked up the bottle... "Damn Bazil... all I wanted was some wine... why couldn't you just let me get a glass of wine?" I said as I curled up into a ball and cried like a baby.

# Chapter 12

"Good morning Mrs. Osgood," Sonia said as I came to the window.

"Good morning."

"What can I do for you today?"

"I need to transfer $2,000 into this account," I replied as I gave her a transfer slip."

"Is you husband okay with this transfer?"

"Is my name on the account?"

"Yes it is Mrs. Osgood."

"Well then... I guess it's okay isn't it?" I snapped...

"I'm sorry..."

"I'm sorry Sonia... I know you're just doing your job... I'm just not having a good day," I said as tears started streaming down my face.

"Come inside Mrs. Osgood," Sonia said as she got up from behind the teller window, put her arm around me, and handed me tissues. "Would you like some coffee?" she asked as she sat down beside me...

"Actually... I'd like something stronger," I sniffed.

"Well... I can take an early lunch and we can go to Fridays if you like... it's always happy hour over there," she laughed.

"That's nice of you... but it isn't necessary..."

"Nonsense Mrs. Osgood... I'll take care of your transfer request... and then we're going to lunch," she said as we left her office. "You're all set Mrs. Osgood... let's go," she ordered by waving her hand towards the door as she held it open...

"I don't want you to get in any trouble..."

"I can do anything I need to do to keep Mr. Osgood happy," she laughed. I couldn't hold it in any longer...

"Mrs. Osgood... c'mon... let's get you that drink," she said as she hurried me across the street to Fridays... "Hold on a minute... Yes Mr. Cochran... I'm with Mrs. Osgood... okay... that's fine..." she said as she hung up.

"Good morning, my name is Latasha and I'll be your server... how may I help you?"

"I'll have a Long Island Ice Tea," I answered.

"Isn't it a little early for that?" Latasha laughed. Sonia looked at me pleading for me not to curse Latasha out but she had nothing to worry about...

"Hell no it isn't too early – it's always 5 o'clock somewhere!" I laughed.

"I'll have an Irish coffee," Sonia said.

"I'll be right back with your drinks ladies," Latasha said as she walked away.

"Mrs. Osgood... I don't mean to pry... but you seemed visibly upset..."

"I don't know where to start," I said as I started crying again...

"Start anywhere you like," Sonia said as she touched my hand...

"Bazil cheated on me," I whispered.

"Figures," she sighed.

"It figures?"

"This is why I don't deal with men..."

"What do you mean?"

"I only deal with women Mrs. Osgood."

"Are you a lesbian?"

"Yes I am... by choice... not by birth..."

"Why?"

"Mrs. Osgood... I love men... but as much as they love you... they always hurt you... they can't help it... it's in their nature... they're just built that way.."

"I love him so much," I whispered as I started crying again...

"He loves you too Mrs. Osgood... he's just a man..."

"What did I do wrong?" I sniffed.

"Nothing Mrs. Osgood... it isn't about you... it's about him..."

"It's about him alright," I said as I took a gulp of my Long Island Ice Tea as soon as Latasha placed the drinks on the table.

"That's right Honey," Sonia agreed as she sipped her coffee.

"Will there be anything else ladies?" Latasha asked.

"No thank you," Sonia answered... "I watched my father cheat on my mother over and over again as I was growing up," Sonia said.

"Really?"

"My mother would sit and cry, walk around depressed, and put him out... just to turn around and take him back!" Sonia snapped. "I got tired of it and I swore on my life that no man would ever put me through that shit!" she said as she banged on the table...

"So... you're a virgin?"

"To men... yes... to The Extreme... no," she laughed.

"The Extreme?"

"My dildo," she laughed.

"Oh my God!"

"Oh please Mrs. Osgood... don't act like you've never used one..."

"I haven't..."

"Oh so you've never masturbated?"

"I never said that," I laughed as I finished my drink...

"Would you ladies like refills?" Latasha asked...

"Hell yea!" I laughed as I began feeling my drink...

"Feeling better?" Sonia asked...

"No... not really," I answered as Latasha brought us our drinks...

"Well... I can't tell you what to do... but if it were me... I wouldn't tolerate it," Sonia said as she sipped her coffee...

"I didn't tolerate it... that's why I needed some money transferred this morning..."

"My Girl! That's what I'm talking about... shit... you need me to transfer some more?"

"No... I just needed enough to cover the mortgage..."

"Mr. Osgood has you paying his mortgage?"

"Not his mortgage... mine..."

"Yours? You mean you have your own house?"

"Damn right I do!" I said as I slammed my hand on the table.

"Are you going to leave him?"

"I already did..."

"Yes Honey! I wish my mom would've had your strength..."

"Don't be so hard on your mom Sonia," I said.

"Why not?"

"Because I'm more like your mother than you realize..."

"Damn Mrs. Osgood... is the dick that good?"

"To be honest... yes..."

"Mrs. Osgood... please tell me that's not all there is to it..."

"Sonia... I wish I could make you understand..."

"Try... I'm listening..."

"I've never felt this way about any other man... that's why I married him as soon as I did... he saved my life... and I couldn't let him go... and I didn't want to... and even though he cheated on my with Trevor... I still can't..."

"What did you just say?"

"Ooopppsss..."

"Mr. Osgood cheated on you... with a man?"

"Yes..."

"I don't get it... why do you still want him?"

"Because I do..."

"You're better than me... I would a killed a mutha fucka..."

"I almost did..."

"What? When?"

"Last night..."

"Mrs. Osgood... What happened?"

"We got into a fight..."

"Because he cheated on you?"

"No... because I got revenge..."

"Now that's what I'm talkin' about!" Sonia yelled as she banged her fist on the table... "Was it somebody he knew?"

"Yes..."

"I'm starting to like you a lot Mrs. Osgood... who was it? Was it his best friend?"

"Actually... Trevor is his best friend..."

"What!?"

"Ssshhh... keep your voice down!"

"Wait... wait... wait... you and your husband fucked the same man?"

"Yes..."

"Damn Mrs. Osgood... this could be a fuckin' movie..."

"I know..."

"So wait a minute... you got into a fight... because you fucked his man?"

"That's part of it..."

"Girl... don't stop now... tell me..."

"He wouldn't let me leave..."

"Oooohhh... now I get it... see... typical male bullshit... I'm glad you left..."

"I'm glad I left too... but I'm miserable without him..."

"I still don't understand how you could want him after all this... but hey... the heart wants what the heart wants... at least that's why my mother used to say..."

"I know how your mother feels..."

"I guess you do..."

"Can I ask you a personal question?"

"More personal than what I just told you?"

"You have a point," Sonia laughed...

"Sure," I said.

"Was it good?"

"Was what good?"

"Trevor..."

"He's alright... but he ain't Bazil!" I laughed.

"Oh shit! So you fucked him for nothing?"

"Not really..."

"So..."

"Why'd I do it?"

"Yea..."

"I did it to hurt Bazil..."

"And now you feel like shit..."

"Exactly..."

"Can I ask you another question?"

"Sure..."

"Have you ever been with a woman?"

"Not intimately... why?"

"Well... have you ever thought about it?"

"Honestly?"

"Yes..."

"I'm strictly dickly," I laughed, "but I've had my curiosity peaked once or twice..."

"By anyone in particular?"

"By porn," I laughed.

"Well... if you're interested... I can make you feel better..."

"I don't know Sonia..."

"Having a sexual experience with a woman doesn't turn you into a lesbian... but it will broaden your horizon... and your pleasure," she laughed.

"We'll see about that," I said as I took her face in my hands and kissed her.

"Mrs. Osgood... I wasn't expecting that," she blushed.

"Neither was I," I smiled.

"Here's my number..." Sonia said as she wrote her number down on a napkin and slipped it to me...

"Okay," I squealed. I couldn't believe I was actually entertaining going through with this... "I feel like I'm back in high school and my crush just gave me his phone number," I giggled.

"Shoot... there goes my phone... let me get back to the bank... call me later..." Sonia said as she paid the check and hurried out...

# Chapter 13

It was Friday night. I'd been coming to Sonia's house every night since last Saturday... and I was enjoying it... but as good as Sonia made me feel, she was making me ache for Bazil..."Don't stop... that's it... right there...," I moaned. She was good. She had me squirting like Bazil never did. I lay there with her for a few moments, and then I got up and went into the living room. Sonia followed behind me and sat down on the couch as she watched me get dressed... "You're leaving aren't you?"

"Yes Sonia."

"I mean... for good..."

"Yes Sonia... for good."

"Why? What did I do?" she asked with tears in her eyes...

"Sonia... c'mere..." I said as I pulled her into a kiss... "You didn't do anything. You're so beautiful... you deserve to be happy... but it can't be with me..."

"Why not? Don't you love me?"

"Sonia... I care about you... more than I've ever cared for any other woman in my life... but I want Bazil..."

"How could you? He'll just hurt you again..."

"I'm willing to take that chance..."

"Why not take a chance with me?"

"Sonia... if I continue to do this with you..."

"You'll be happy... I know you will..."

"Sonia... yes... I'm very happy when I'm with you..."

"So why are you throwing it all away?"

"Sonia... I love Bazil... I want Bazil..."

"So what was this then?"

"This..." I answered as I pulled her into a deep kiss... "Was... a... wonderful.... incredible... exhilarating... experience I'll never forget... but I want Bazil... I need Bazil..."

"Will I ever see you again?"

"The door's open..." I answered as I left. As soon as I got in a cab, I called Bazil. "Oh good – voicemail..." I breathed...

"Hey my Thirst Quencher.. I'm glad you didn't answer the phone because I can say what I want to say without you interrupting me with kisses... or anything else. I love you... I miss you... I want you... I need you... I'm coming home... I'll see you later..."

# Punishment

"My Thirst Quencher," I breathed as Bazil pulled me into a deep, passionate kiss...

"Beautiee..." he moaned in between kisses....

"I missed you so much..."

"I missed you too..."

"What's wrong Bazil? Aren't you happy to see me?"

"Very..."

"What's wrong then?"

"You left me Beautiee..."

"You hurt me Bazil..."

"I know... and I'm sorry..." he said as he pushed me away from him... "But you need to be punished..."

"Punished? For what?" I snapped...

"For denying me pussy..."

"Oooohhhh..." I breathed. The thought of being punished turned me on... and Bazil knew it...

"Come with me," Bazil commanded as he took me by the hand and led me upstairs to the bedroom... "Take off your clothes..." Bazil commanded... "Come here to me..." he commanded as he watched me walk towards him... "Undress me... slowly..."

"Yes my Thirst Quencher," I said as I began undressing him. I took my time sliding his shirt off his shoulders and down his arms... "Damn you smell good," I moaned as I began kissing him down his chest...

"Stop..." Bazil commanded... "Go sit on the edge of the bed..."

"Okay!" I squealed. I sat on the bed and watched Bazil come towards me. Once he was standing in front of me he picked my head up by my chin...

"Who am I?"

"My Thirst Quencher..." I breathed. Bazil unbuckled his belt, dropped his pants, and stood before me with his dick directly in front of me...

"Open your mouth..." he commanded as I opened my mouth... "Quench your Thirst..." he commanded as he slowly placed his dick in my mouth... "Yeeesss.... Beautiee..." Bazil moaned as I quenched my thirst... "MmmmMmmmmmm..... That's it... suck it..." he moaned as he grabbed me by the head and pushed his dick in deeper... "I'm about to cumm.... Beautiee.... Beautiee..." he moaned as I swallowed him... "Shhiittt.... Fuck.... Fuck... Fuck.... Aaaaaaggghhhh!" He continued to stand there and let me suck his dick for a few moments until he spoke... "I'm not done with you..."

"I know..."

"Lay back... and spread your legs..."

"Yes my Thirst Quencher..." I breathed as I did as I was told...

"Mmmmmm..." he moaned... "Look at my pretty pussy..." he breathed as he slid two fingers inside me, pulled them out, and licked them... "You taste different," he said as he licked his fingers... "Damn you're so wet..." he breathed as he got on his knees, slid his hands under my ass, pulled me to the edge, spread my legs... and dove in...

"Bazil..." I moaned as he began licking, sucking, and slurping...

"Mmmmmm... you taste sweeter than before..." he breathed as he slipped his tongue inside me...

"Oh Bazil..." I moaned as he swirled his tongue inside, then spread my lips and began sucking... "Bazziiiilll!" I screamed as I arched my back and I came in his mouth... "Mmmmmm... you taste so good..." he breathed as he continued licking and sucking... "So... Beautiee... who is she?"

"Whhhaaattt?" I asked as I tried to sit up but Bazil pushed me back down on the bed, continuing to lick and suck...

"Who is she?"

"How did you know?" I breathed as I grabbed his head and pushed him down between my legs...

114

"Once... a... woman... experiences... an... orgasm... with... another... woman... she... changes... for... the... better..." he moaned as he picked up the pace...

"Ohhhh.... Bazzziiilll..." I moaned as I started riding his face... "How?"

"There's... something... about... a... woman's... tongue... that... brings... out... the... sweetest... nectar... from... the... pussy..." Bazil moaned as he continued sucking...

"Bazil... Bazil... Bazil..." I moaned as he slid his hands under my ass and buried his head further and his tongue deeper...
"Aaaagggghhhh.... Aaaagggghhhh.... Aaaagggghhhh!" I screamed before collapsing on the bed. I watched as Bazil stood up, climbed up on the bed, and lay on top of me...

"Taste yourself," he commanded as he pulled me into a deep kiss, slipping his tongue inside as he covered my mouth complete...

"Mmmmmm......" I moaned as I enjoyed the taste...

"So..." Bazil asked as he slid himself inside me and began thrusting... "Who... is... she?"

"Sonia!" I moaned...

"From... the... bank?"

"Yyyeeessss!" I moaned.

"Did... she... fuck... you?"

"Nooo..... Bazil..." I moaned.

"Did... you... miss... me?"

"Yeeesss! Ooohhh... Bazziilll..."

"You... need... to... be... taught... a... lesson..." Bazil growled as he began thrusting harder and faster...

"Bazil... Bazil... Bazzziiilll!" I screamed...

"Yessss Beautiee... who's... pussy... is... this..."

"Yooouuurrrsss!" I screamed as I came again. Bazil continued thrusting until my orgasm subsided and then got up off of me...

"Get up and turn your ass towards me..." he commanded. I did as I was told and as I did I could feel the tip of Bazil's dick on my ass... "Grab the headboard and hold on..." Bazil commanded... "Spread your legs..." Bazil commanded... "May I?" Bazil whispered in my ear as he slipped on a condom and lotioned it with Vaseline. I could feel the tip of his dick on my ass as he laid himself on my back...

"I don't know Bazil..."

"Please Beautiee..." he whispered in my ear as he began playing with my pussy...

"Ooohhh... that feels good..."

"This will too... I promise..."

"Okay..." I breathed... trembling...

"Relax Beautiee... I won't hurt you..." he whispered as he slowly began inserting himself in my ass...

"MmmmMmmm..." I moaned as he continued playing with my pussy while going in further...

"Are you okay?" he asked as he began thrusting...

"Oh Bazil..." I moaned as I began to enjoy sensations from Bazil indirectly hitting my G spot. Bazil stopped playing with my pussy and pulled me close to him, breathing heavy in my ear, still thrusting... "Bazil... I'm gonna cummmm..." I moaned...

"I'm cumming with you Beautiee..." he growled in my ear as he began thrusting deeper...

"Bazil... Bazil... Bazil..."

"Beautiee... Beautiee.... Beautiee...."

"Aaaagggghhhh!" We both collapsed on the bed while Bazil was still inside me... "Beautiee..." he whispered in my ear while kissing my neck...

"Bazil..." I moaned...

"Turn over Beautiee..." Bazil commanded as he slid out my ass, took off the condom, dropped it on the floor, climbed on top of me, pinned my hands above my head with his, spread my legs with his knee, and slid back inside me... "Listen to me Beautiee..." he breathed as he began thrusting...

"Yes my Thirst Quencher..." I moaned as Bazil began kissing me on my neck and earlobe...

"If... you... ever... leave... me... again... I'll... fuck... you... to... death... do... you... understand... me?"

"Yeeessss Bazil.... Yeeessss!" I moaned...

"Mmmmmm..... good..."

# Chapter 15

"Good morning..." Bazil said as he woke me up, kissing me and messaging my breasts...

"Yesss... it... is..." I moaned as he moved his hand from my breasts to my body...

"I missed you Beatuiee..." he moaned...

"I missed you too..."

"Even though you were with Sonia?" he asked as he propped himself up on his elbow to look down at me while continuing to touch me all over...

"Yeesss..." I moaned, closing my eyes...

"I cried when you left..." he said, tearing up. I opened my eyes and saw his were filling with tears... and so were mine...

"Oh Bazil..." I said as I kissed tears off his face... "I love you sooo much... please don't cry," I said as I started crying too...

"If you stop... I'll stop..." he said as he kissed me fully..."

"I cried too..."

"You did?" he asked with relief in his voice...

"Yes Bazil..."

"I'm sorry Beautiee..." he said as he kissed me and I could feel his tears...

"I'm sorry too..." I said as I started crying...

"You have nothing to be sorry for Beautiee..."

"Yes Bazil... I do..."

"No Beautiee..."

"Bazil... listen to me..."

"Okay..."

"I know it hurt you when I left you... and I'm sorry..."

"I didn't give you a choice..."

"Bazil?"

"Yesss..."

"Can we talk?"

"Okay..." he sighed. "I'll go make breakfast... and coffee..." he said as he got up out of bed. When he reached for his boxers I stopped him...

"Bazil?"

"Yes?"

"Leave your boxers here... it's been a while since I've seen you in all your glory..."

"It's chilly..."

"Put on your robe... but leave it open slightly... so I can enjoy the view..."

"Okay..." he smiled as he put on his robe, leaving it slightly open, and went downstairs to make breakfast. I got up out of bed when I started to smell coffee, put on my robe, and went downstairs to the kitchen...

"Just in time Beautiee..." he said as he handed me a cup of coffee with hazelnut creamer...

"Mmmmm.... I missed this..." I moaned.

"You didn't have coffee?"

"I didn't have your coffee," I said as I pulled him into a kiss. "Mmmmmm..." I moaned as I pulled him to me, slid my hand inside his robe, and grabbed his ass...

"Mmmmmm...." He moaned as my robe fell open and he pressed his dick up against me...

"I need to finish my coffee," I laughed as I stopped.

"Hmmmm.... alright," he said as he sat down at the table with a cup of coffee for himself...

"Can I ask you something Bazil?"

"Sure."

"Have you always... you know..."

"Am I gay?"

"Yes."

"No..."

"I'm confused..."

"Let me explain..."

"Okay..."

"As I told you, I met Trevor in prison and we hit it off..."

"Okay..."

"I was good for a while... but..."

"It's okay Bazil... tell me..." I said as I got up from the table, walked over to him, and put my arm around him...

"I don't want to hurt you Beautiee..."

"I know Bazil... it's okay..."

"One night I was jacking off... he caught me... and one thing led to another..."

"I understand Bazil..."

"How can you understand it Beautiee? I don't even understand it..."

"You're a man... you have needs..."

"It went like that for a while... but..."

"But you caught feelings..."

"Yea... I know I shouldn't have... but I did... I tried not too..."

"You love him don't you?"

"Yes Beautiee..." he whispered with tears in his eyes...

"Why me?"

"I always wanted to get married... like I said... I'm not gay..."

"How does Trevor feel about that?"

"He hates it... but I'll never be that for him... especially now that I have you..."

"Bazil?"

"Yes Beautiee?"

"We're you ever going to tell me about him?"

"Yes Beautiee..."

"What you did was selfish..."

"I know..."

121

"You made me love you so I couldn't leave... even if I wanted to..."

"I know... I'm sorry..."

"I know you are... but I have to be honest..."

"Yes Beautiee?"

"I can't lose you," I said with tears in my eyes..."

"Oh Beautiee..." Bazil cried as he pulled me into a kiss... "Never... I promise..." he cried as he kissed me again and again... "I'll tell him it's over...

"You will?"

"Yes Beautiee..."

"Oh Bazil..." I cried harder... "I love you sooo much..."

"I love you too..."

"Are you sure? I know you love him..."

"Yes... I do love him... but you're my wife... I hurt you... you came back to me... and you still want me... I love you..." he cried as he pulled me into a kiss..."

"Stop Bazil..."

"What's wrong?"

"I need to tell you something..."

"Okay..."

"I went to fuck him to hurt you..."

"I know..."

"I'm sorry..."

"Can I ask you something Beautiee?"

"Yes..."

"Did you... umm..."

"Hell no!" I saw the relief on Bazil's face but I didn't say anything...

"I went to see Trevor after Katina left..."

"Did you fuck him?" Bazil didn't bother to answer... he just turned his head away from me... "Bazil?"

"Yes Beautiee?"

"Why was Katina here?"

"We fought."

"Bazil?"

"Yes Beautiee?"

"Why was Katina here?"

"Katina is a detective from the Special Investigations Unit in Milford, Connecticut. She was the detective who arrested me...Beautiee?"

"Yes Bazil?"

"Was Sonia your first?"

"Yes."

"What made you... you know..."

"I told her what happened between us..."

"Why?"

"I went to transfer money... we exchanged words... one thing led to another... I started crying... she brought me into her office and offered me coffee but I said I wanted something stronger... then she took me out for drinks..."

"I'm sorry Beautiee..."

"I know..."

"So how did... you know..."

"We started drinking... and talking... she told me that's why she's never been with a man and she only deals with women..."

"Really?"

"Yes..."

"So how did you..."

"She asked me if I had ever been with a woman... I told her I hadn't but I was curious... she said if I was interested she might be able to make me feel better... so I kissed her..."

"Oh my..." Bazil breathed... I could tell this was exciting him... especially when he got up from the table, came over to me, pulled me up, turned me around, moved my robe, and bent me over... "Did she eat you?" he breathed as he slid inside me and started thrusting..."

"Yeeesss..." I moaned as I spread my legs and grabbed the table...

"Where did you do it?"

"On her deck..." I moaned...

"Did you cum?"

"Oh yesss..." I moaned...

"How many times did you cum?"

"Three..." I moaned...

"Did you eat her too?" he asked as he thrust harder...

"Yeessss..." I moaned...

"Did you make her come?"

"Yeesss! Yeesss!" I moaned...

"Did you enjoy it?"

"Yes Bazil... Yeessss!" I screamed as I came... but he wasn't finished...

"I want you to invite her over... so I can watch..." he breathed as he pulled me closer and whispered in my ear as he continued thrusting... "I want to watch you come!" he growled...

"Oh Bazil!" I moaned...

"Cum for me again!" he growled as he thrust harder and deeper...

"Baaazzziiilll!" I screamed as my legs trembled...

"MmmmMmmmph... MmmmMmmmph... MmmmMmmmph! Oh shiiittt... I'm cummin... Aaaaggghhh!" he continued thrusting... slowing his pace, but not stopping... I want to watch her make you cum," he breathed as he turned me around, pulled me to him, and kissed me deeply...

"Yes my Thirst Quencher... yes..." I breathed as we slowly stopped kissing...

"Sit down... I'll make breakfast now..." he breathed as he took the food out of the fridge... "So... how long did it last?" Bazil asked as he scrambled the eggs for the omelet...

"How many days was I gone?"

"About a week..."

"That long..."

"So... did you spend the night?"

"No."

"Why not?" Bazil asked as he put the turkey bacon in the frying pan...

"I didn't want to... I wanted to go home..."

125

"There's something you're not telling me..."

"Yes..."

"Did something happen Beautiee?" he asked as he came over to me and put his arm around me...

"Yea..."

"What happened?"

"Bazil... I never wanted to spend the night... I wanted to go home..."

"Damn..." Bazil laughed as he went to take the bacon out of the pan and start cooking the omelets... "You just wanted to bust a nut and bounce..."

"Yea..."

"I still don't understand why you never spent the night..."

"What does it matter?"

"I'm sorry... I'll stop asking..." he said as he put the bacon and omelets on plates, got forks, brought them to the table and asked again... "What happened?"

"I started thinking about you..."

"You did?"

"Yea..."

"That's sweet," he said as he leaned in to kiss me... "So... you didn't enjoy being with her?"

"Yes... she made me feel good... and she felt good too..."

"What was it like when you... ate her pussy... did you like it?'

"Yes... I liked it... a lot..."

126

"I see..." he said as he rubbed his chin in thought...

"She spoke Spanish then too..."

"Damn Beautiee... she thought she was turning you out but you ended up turning her out," he laughed.

"You're right," I laughed. "She kept asking me if I was sure I've never done it before..."

"Have you?"

"No Bazil..."

"Beautiee? Beautiee?"

"Oh... sorry... I was just thinking..."

"About what?"

"About Sonia..." I sighed.

"I can't wait to watch you..." Bazil breathed.

"I hope she's willing..."

"She won't give you any trouble..."

"What makes you so sure?"

"She's feeling you... big time..."

"Naaa..."

"Trust me Beautiee... she's feeling you..."

"Okay... if you say so..." I said as I got up from the table and yawned... "I'm going back to bed..."

"I know so..." Bazil said as he followed me back upstairs...

# Chapter 16

"Hey Sonia," I said as I walked into the bank.

"Mrs. Osgood!" Mr. Cochran said when he saw me... "Nice to see you!"

"It's nice to see you too Mr. Cochran," I replied.

"Sonia?" I asked...

"Yes Mrs. Osgood?"

"May we speak in private?"

"Sure..." she said as we went into her office and closed the door... "How can I help you Mrs. Osgood," Sonia sighed as she sat down...

"What's wrong Sonia?"

"Nothing... its' just been one of those days," she sighed.

"Well... I said as I stepped closer to her... "I came here to ask you something..."

"Okay..." she said as I began massaging her shoulders...

"Please stop..."

"Okay..." I said as I moved away from her and sat down across from her...

"What do you need?"

"Right now I need for you to tell me why you're upset with me..." I said.

"I'm sorry Mrs. Osgood... its' just that I'm at work..."

"Okay... Well... I wanted to ask you something..."

"Yes Mrs. Osgood?"

"I told my husband about us..."

"Us? There is no us... you made that perfectly clear..."

"You're right... but I also said the door's open..."

"Are you saying you'd like to see me again?"

"I'm saying we'd like to see you..."

"Excuse me?"

"I told my husband about us... and told him how much I enjoyed being with you..."

"You enjoyed being with me?"

"Yes Sonia... I enjoyed being with you..."

"I enjoyed being with you too..." she said as she touched my hand... "But what's this got to do with your husband?"

"Well... he wants you to come to the house and make love to me... while he watches...

"Mrs. Osgood... I'm not sure that's a good idea..."

"Why not?"

"That can get very messy... and I don't do messy..."

"He just wants to watch..."

"He's a man with a dick... he'll watch... and then he'll want to join in..."

"I don't understand... you use a dildo..."

"Yes Mrs. Osgood - I use a dildo – because a dildo isn't attached to anyone or anything – there's no feelings involved – it does what I need it to do, then it goes back in the drawer – and it doesn't come back out until I need it again – and it will never, ever, control me..."

"Is that what you think my husband does to me?"

"That's what all men do Mrs. Osgood – that's why I have no desire to be with a man..."

"My husband's not controlling me..."

"Mrs. Osgood - you're here – asking me to have a threesome with you and your husband – because it's what your husband wants – if that's not control – then what is it?"

"Yes Sonia... my husband did ask me to invite you to our bedroom... but I'm here because I want to be..."

"So... you want me to have a threesome with you and your husband?"

"No Sonia..."

"Well then... what do you want?"

"Well... when my husband asked me if I enjoyed you... I told him I did. He asked me how many times you made me cum... so when he said he wanted to watch you make me cum... the thought of him watching turned me on..."

"Wow... you are something else Mrs. Osgood..."

"I'll take that as a compliment..." I laughed.

"I didn't really mean it that way..."

"So what do you mean?"

"I'm glad I turn you on... but do you really believe your husband just wants to watch?"

"No..."

"Okay then... so you understand why I don't think it's a good idea..."

"Yes... I understand..."

"It's better if we don't start something that could lead to nothing but problems..."

"I guess you're right..."

"Can I ask you something?"

"Sure..."

"If I said yes..."

"Okay..."

"What if your husband wanted to join in? How would you feel about that?"

"Well... honestly... since I slept with you... I guess I'd be okay with it..."

"So... you come here to ask me to have a threesome with you and your husband... and you're not sure how you feel about it?"

"Well... yea..."

"Let me ask you this... what if I fuck your husband... and I like it?"

"This is so easy when you're watching porn..." I sighed.

"Exactly — they don't show you what happens when the camera goes off. Did you know most porn stars are either single or married to another porn star?"

"No."

"Why do you think that is?"

"Because... I can't imagine going home to Bazil and saying not tonight honey... I've been fucking all day," I laughed.

"I just want you to understand what you're asking me..."

"I do..."

"There's something I need to tell you Mrs. Osgood..."

"Yes?"

"Please don't be upset..."

"Okay..."

"I enjoyed being with you... but I couldn't fuck your husband if I wanted to... and trust me... I don't want to..."

"Did something happen between you and my husband?"

"No Mrs. Osgood..."

"Oh thank God," I breathed."

"See? That's what I mean — you're relieved nothing happened between us — but you're here asking me to fuck him..."

"Sonia..."

"What?" she snapped.

"I'm not relieved nothing happened between you... I'm relieved he didn't hurt you..."

132

"Why would you think he'd hurt me?"

"I can see it in your face..."

"What you see is anger..."

"Because I went back to him?"

"Because he's just like my father – he uses women then tosses them when he's done with them unless they leave him first..."

"How do you know so much about my husband?"

"Forget it... I shouldn't have said anything..."

"It's a little late for that Sonia..." I said as I got up to leave...

"Beautiee... wait... please..." she said as she pulled me into a kiss...

"Have a good day Sonia..." I said as I opened the door, walked out her office, and out the bank.

# Chapter 17

"Beautiee..." Bazil said as he pulled me into a kiss...

"Hey my Thirst Quencher..." I sighed.

"What's wrong?"

"I'm just tired..." I lied.

"Beautiee..." he whispered in my ear as he began massaging my shoulders... "You're lying... please don't lie to me..." he said as he started kissing me on my neck...

"Mmmmmm... that feels nice..."

"Beautiee... tell me..."

"Okay..." I breathed as I turned around and pulled Bazil into a kiss...

"Mmmmmm... I know what you're up to..." Bazil moaned...

"I know what you're up to... too..." I moaned as I began massaging his dick through his pants...

"Come with me," Bazil commanded as he took me into the living room, laid down on the couch, and pulled me down on top of him... "Mmmmmm..." he moaned as I loosened his belt and released his dick from his pants...

134

"Mmmmmm..." I moaned as I lifted my skirt and slid down on his dick...

"Mmmmmph...           Mmmmmph... Mmmmmph..." Bazil moaned as I rode his dick...

"Bazil... Fuck!" I moaned as I pushed myself up with my hands and continued riding...

"Umph... Umph... Umph..." Bazil growled as he grabbed me by the waist and began thrusting...

"Bazil... I'm cummmmmmiiiinnnnggg.... I'm cummmmmmiiiinnnnggg...."

"Oh shit... fuuuuccckkkkk!" Bazil growled as I collapsed on top of him...

Bazil..." I breathed... "That was so fuckin' good..."

"Indeed..." Bazil breathed as he held me...

"I need to tell you something Bazil..."

"I know..."

"You do?"

"Yes Beautiee..."

"How did you know?"

"I saw it in your face..."

"Why didn't you stop me?"

"Because..." he said as he kissed me... "Your... face... is... beautiful... when... you... cum..."

"Oh Bazil... I love you..."

"I love you too..."

"I went to see Sonia today..."

"You did?"

"Yes Bazil..."

"What happened?"

"She doesn't think it's a good idea..."

"HhhMmmmmm... did she say why?"

"She gave me lots of reasons – she asked me if I would be okay if she fucked you... and liked it..."

"Would you?"

"To be honest... I don't know..."

"Is that why you were so upset?"

"No..."

"There's something else?"

"Yes..."

"Okay..."

"She said she couldn't fuck you if she wanted to because you're too much like her father..." I could feel Bazil tense up immediately...

"What else did she say?" he asked as he sat up a little...

"She said you use women and toss them aside when you're done with them... unless they leave you first..." Bazil was so angry his body got hard... "Did something happen between you and Sonia that you haven't told me?" I asked with tears in my eyes...

"Come here Beautiee..." he said as he sat up... "Sonia and I have known each other for a long time..."

"You have?"

"Yes Beautiee. When I first met Sonia she told me about her father... and she asked for my help..."

"So you helped her?"

"Yes Beautiee..."

"Did anything else ever happen between you?"

"Yes... and no..."

"What does that mean?"

"She needed a job so I spoke to Mr. Cochran on her behalf. We went out a few times – we kissed – we touched – but that's as far as it went..."

"Did you ever hurt her?" I asked with tears in my eyes, pleading for him to tell me he hadn't...

"Beautiee..."

"Yes Bazil?"

"I've never hurt Sonia... or any other woman..." he answered.

"She told me that..."

"She did?"

"Yes."

"So why was she so angry today?"

"Because... I went to see her..."

"You did?"

"Yes..."

"When?"

"After you told me what happened between you..."

"Were you angry?"

"No Beautiee... I was turned on when you told me what happened... remember?"

"Yes... I remember..."

"I went to invite her to come here... so I could watch..."

"Did she get angry?"

"Actually... she seemed open to the idea..."

"Well... after what happened today... she's closed..."

"Give her time... she'll calm down..."

"She said I was there because you were controlling me... with your dick..." I laughed.

"You know what? That's funny – especially because you left me to be with her – my dick had nothing to do with it," he laughed.

"I told her I was there because the thought of you watching me turned me on..."

"Don't worry about it Beautiee..."

"I'm not... not anymore..." I sighed as I snuggled up next to Bazil.

# Chapter 18

"Hello Sonia..." I said loud enough for Bazil to hear as I answered my cell...

"Hey Beautiee..." Sonia said as I put the phone on speaker... "I just wanted to call and apologize for what happened earlier...

"You don't need to apologize Sonia..."

"Yes Beautiee... I do..."

"I'm sorry I made you uncomfortable..."

"I was just taken aback..."

"I understand Sonia..."

"Let me explain Beautiee..."

"Okay..."

"I've never been with a married woman before..."

"Ooohhh..."

"Before you, I was only with single women... no strings... sometimes they wanted a relationship... sometimes they wanted sex... sometimes they wanted others... but it was always just between us..."

"Uh huh..."

"Then you came along... I knew you were married... I never should have suggested anything in the first place... but you were in bad shape and I wanted... needed... to comfort you..."

"Oh Sonia! How Sweet!" I exclaimed as Bazil's face lit up...

"Once you kissed me... which I never expected... I was done..."

"I didn't plan that... it just happened..."

"I could tell it was genuine... you're so sweet..."

"Aawwww... thank you Sonia..." I said as Bazil pulled me closer...

"I fell in love with you Beautiee... I know I shouldn't have... but I couldn't help it..." she said to Bazil's delight...

"I'm sorry if I led you on Sonia... I didn't mean to..."

"I know you didn't Beautiee..."

"I care about you... but I love Bazil..."

"As you should... he's your husband... that's why when you invited me to your home I freaked out... I can't be the other woman in your marriage..."

"I'm sorry Sonia... I never meant to make you feel that way..."

"I know you didn't Beautiee... how could you know... you've never done anything like this before..."

"It looks so easy in porn..."

"As I said – they're actors – and they never show you what happens when the cameras go off..."

"Well... you did ask me if you'd ever see me again..."

"Yes I did..."

"And I told you the door was open..."

"Yes you did..."

"So... when someone opens the door for you... isn't it rude not to come in?"

"Beautiee... I can't with you..." she laughed.

"I understand how you feel Sonia... it's just that I've always fantasized about..."

"About what Beautiee?" Sonia asked as Bazil looked at me perplexed, waiting for me to answer...

"I've always fantasized about being with a woman... and getting caught by my husband... and him joining in..." I answered as Bazil beamed...

"Oh wow... I had no idea..."

"I've never told anyone that before..."

"I feel honored you shared that with me..."

"I've never been with a woman before and since I've been with you... as you said... I've broadened my horizon... and my orgasms..."

"Awww... Damn Beautiee... you about to make me cry..."

"I'll tell you something else Sonia..."

"What's that?"

"Bazil says since I've been with you... I taste sweeter..."

"Okay Beautiee... okay... enough already... I'll do it... just once..."

"You will?"

"Yes Beautiee... I'll do it... but I do have two conditions..."

"Yes Sonia?"

"Number one... your husband can watch... but if he joins in, he's not to touch me..."

"Okay..."

"Number two... I'm expecting that you will make love to me as well..."

"I'm looking forward to it Sonia..."

"Are you?"

"Yeeesss..."

"Okay Beautiee... how's Friday night at 8:00 p.m.?"

"Perfect..." I said as Bazil kissed me...

"Do I need to bring anything?"

"No Sonia..."

"Okay... I'll see you both Friday night..."

# Chapter 19

"Come in Sonia..." I said as I opened the door...

"Hi Beautiee..." Sonia said as she came in and closed the door behind her... leaving it slightly cracked...

"Come with me..." I said as I took her by the hand and walker her into the kitchen...

"Your home is lovely..."

"Thank you..." I said as I shooed Bazil away from the doorway, opened the wine, and poured two glasses... "Moscato?"

" Yes... thank you..." she said as we both started drinking...

"Sonia... I'm nervous as hell..." I whispered...

"Oh thank God..." she laughed... "I thought it was just me..."

"I remember you gave me wine on our first night together..." I said as I went towards her...

"Yes... I did..." she said as she pulled me into a kiss...

"Mmmmmm...." I moaned as she slipped her tongue in my mouth. I could see Bazil watching us from the corner of my eye and it turned me on. We finished our wine, put our glasses down on the island, and continued kissing each other for a few minutes until I spoke... "C'mon Sonia... let's go upstairs..."

"Okay..." she said as she followed me upstairs, down the hall, and into our bedroom... "Oh wow... you have a lovely suite..."

"Thank you..."

"So... shall I sit?" she asked as she patted the bed...

"Please..." I said as I sat down beside her... "I can't believe I'm doing this..." I whispered...

"Hmmmmm... neither can I..." she said as she began unbuttoning my blouse. I unbuttoned Sonia's blouse and we both slid our blouses off each other's shoulders at the same time. Neither of us was wearing a bra so we both began massaging each other's breasts and started kissing. I saw Bazil watching us, fully naked, from the closet, while he was stroking his dick... and I wanted it...

"Lay down on your back..." I commanded. Sonia lay down and I slid her pants down off of her and tossed them to the floor. I slid my own pants off, tossed them to the floor, and lay between her legs...

"Beautiee...." she moaned as I started sucking her breasts. I started kissing Sonia down her body and continued kissing until I reached her pussy. I put my face down and put my ass up, knowing what Bazil was going to do...

"Ooohhh..." I moaned as Bazil grabbed me by the waist and started fucking me from behind...

"Beautiee... yeeesss....." Sonia moaned as my tongue went up inside her pussy...

"Yeesss..." Bazil moaned as he thrust harder...

"Mmmmmm...." I moaned in Sonia's pussy, licking and sucking with each thrust...

"Make her cum..." Bazil commanded as he fucked me harder...

"Mmmmmm.... MmmmMmmm.... MmmmMmmm....." I moaned into Sonia's pussy as she began riding my face...

"Beautiee... Beautiee... don't stop... don't stop...

"Your pussy is so fuckin' wet..." Bazil growled... Ugggh! Ugggh! Ugggh!"

"Mmmmmm.... Mmmmmm.... Mmmmmm...." I moaned in Sonia's pussy as she grabbed my head...

"Oh shit... fuck... I'm cumming!" Sonia screamed as she clamped her legs around my head and rode my face harder. Bazil was so turned on he took it out on my pussy and my legs began shaking uncontrollably...

"Mmmmmm! Mmmmmm! Mmmmmm! I moaned into Sonia's pussy as her orgasmic wave was coming down her body while my orgasmic

145

wave was going up my body and we both collapsed on top of Sonia...

"UMmmmm... I can't breathe..." Sonia laughed...

"Sorry about that..." Bazil said as he got up off me and stood there looking down at us...

"Are you ready?" Sonia breathed as I kissed her...

"Yes... I'm... ready..." I said in between kisses...

"I really enjoyed that..." Sonia breathed...

"So did I..." Bazil breathed. I could feel Sonia tensing up as she heard Bazil's voice so I tried to make her comfortable...

"I'm glad you enjoyed me Sonia..." I breathed as I kissed her again and she rolled me over on my back.

"Open your legs..." Sonia commanded as she started sucking my breasts...

"Mmmmmm..." I moaned as she kissed her way down my stomach to my pussy...

"Bazil..." I moaned as she started licking, slurping, and sucking. I looked at Bazil and saw how turned on he was... so much so that he started stroking his dick again... "Oh Bazil..." I moaned as she put her tongue inside my pussy, licking, sucking, and slurping from inside, out, and inside again... "Bazil... she's gonna make me cum..." I moaned...

"Mmmmmm..." Bazil moaned as he came over and put his dick in my mouth...

"Mmmmmm.....                    Mmmmmm.....
Mmmmmm....." I moaned on Bazil's dick as Sonia
put her hands up under me, lifted my ass up off
the bed, and dove in... "Baaazzziiilll! Look out!"
I screamed as I saw the gun... but it was too
late...

"Aagggghhhh!" Bazil cried out as he tried
to dodge the bullet... but failed...

"Sonia!" I grabbed her up from between my
legs and held her down on my body to shield us
both but realized what was going on when she got
hit...

"Sonia! Nooooo!" Trevor cried as he
dropped the gun to rush to her... "This is all your
fault Beautiee! She didn't deserve to die!" he
cried...

"She deserved to die... and so do you!" I
screamed as I grabbed the gun before Trevor
could... and pulled the trigger...

"Beautiee! Beautiee! It's Keisha... you
okay in there?"

"Oh God... Baaazzziiillll!" I screamed as I
dropped the gun on the floor...

"Keisha... what's wrong?" her husband
Troy asked as he ran towards our house...

"She needs help... break the door..."

"The police are on their way Keisha – let's
go!"

"Mutha fucka I said break the fuckin'
door... NNNOOOOWWWW!!!"

"Fine – but I ain't payin' for this shit!" he growled as he broke the door down and they came rushing upstairs...

"Beautiee!  Where are you?" Troy yelled...

"I'm in here!" I screamed...

"Oh Shit!  What the fuck... Yo Keisha... we out..."

"Please don't leave me!" I cried...

"Troy – get a robe!" Keisha said as she tried to shield me from her husband...

"Here..." Troy said as he tossed the robe to Keisha...

"Here Beautiee... put this on..." she said as she helped me put on the robe...

"Damn Keisha... you got blood all over your clothes..." Troy said as he shook his head...

"I don't give a fuck about these clothes!" Keisha yelled...

"Oh shit - the cops are here – yo Keisha – lets go!"

"I'm not leaving her Troy – look at her! Damn... I'm sorry Beautiee... are you okay?"

"Bazil... I whispered as I pointed towards Bazil..."

"Is he dead?" Troy asked...

"Step aside sir," the techs from the ambulance said as they pushed their way into the room...

"Bazil..." I said as I pointed towards Bazil...

"We've got a pulse - he's still alive – let's get him to the hospital – stat!" they said as I watched them lift Bazil's bloody unconscious body onto the stretcher...

"Bazil!" I screamed as I ran down the stairs behind them, not bothering to close my robe...

"Maam... are you okay?" one of the techs asked...

"Bazil!" I screamed as I ran out the house following the stretcher... and ran right into Katina Jones...

"Mrs. Osgood – oh my God – what happened?"

"Bazil!" I screamed as I pushed her down and the ambulance closed the door...

"Wait!" the driver said as he saw me running naked... covered in blood... robe swirling behind me...

"Is this your husband maam?" I didn't answer... I just snatched the door open and climbed in... and Keisha was right behind me...

"We got a gunshot!" The paramedics yelled as they rushed in through the ambulance entrance...

"What happened?" a nurse tried to ask me but I followed behind the ambulance techs with Bazil...

"Excuse me Miss, can we get some information from you?" the nurse asked Keisha...

"Bazil Osgood — and that's his wife," Keisha answered as she ran behind me...

"What do we have here?" the doctor asked as he came running out...

"He's been shot... he's stabilized but we can't stop the bleeding..."

"Get him into surgery — stat — and get me Nurse Trinity..." the doctor said as he flew down the hall...

"Mrs. Osgood?"

"Yes?"

"We need you to wait here..." Nurse Trinity said...

"That's my husband!" I screamed as Keisha pulled me into a hug to console me...

"Mrs. Osgood - we need to get your husband into surgery - Dr. Preston's the best - We'll do everything we can!" she said as she rushed off behind Dr. Preston...

"Beautiee... sit down..." Keisha said she held me...

"Okay..." I cried...

"He's gonna make it..." she said reassuringly as she rubbed my hand...

"Mrs. Osgood?" another nurse said as she came up to me...

"Yes?" I answered as I looked up at her...

"Ummmmm..."

"Yes... Yvonne?" I asked as I read her name tag...

"You're naked... and you're both covered in blood...

"Yea..." I said as I stared off into space...."

"Maam?" Nurse Yvonne asked Keisha...

"Yes Nurse?"

"Are you hurt?"

"No," Keisha answered as her husband came running down the hall...

"Keisha!" Troy yelled when he saw her...

"I'm alright Troy," she said as he sat down...

"Mrs. Osgood?"

"Yes Nurse?"

"Can you come with me please?"

"I need to be here when my husband gets out of surgery...."

"Mrs. Osgood... I need you to come with me... please..."

"Why?"

"You're naked... you're covered in blood..."

"You want me to take a shower?" I laughed hysterically...

"I can't let you do that..."

"Excuse me?"

"Mrs. Osgood... your husband was shot... you were on the scene... we need to do a rape kit and get some samples..."

"Keisha... is she for real right now?" I laughed.

"Hell you askin' me for – I'on know!" Keisha laughed.

"My husband didn't rape me!" I snapped…

"Did anyone else rape you?"

"Hell no!"

"Umm… well… Mrs. Osgood… I don't understand… I'm new here… just come with me… please…"

"Okay…" I said as I followed Nurse Yvonne…   "This is Nurse Tisha," Nurse Yvonne explained as I was escorted into another examining room…

"Mrs. Osgood?" Nurse Tisha asked…

"Yes?"

"We need to take some pictures… get some samples… and do a rape kit…" she said as she patted the table for me to sit…

"I wasn't raped…" I said…

"We still need to do a rape kit…"

"You can take your pictures – you can get your samples – but you're not doing a rape kit," I said as I dropped my robe…

"Oh my God – what happened?" she asked as she got the camera and began taking pictures…

"My husband got shot," I answered…

"Did you shoot him?"

"You know what – hurry up with your pictures and your swabs so I can get back to my husband!" I snapped.

"I'm sorry… it's just… never mind…"

"It's just you thought I was an angry woman that caught her husband cheating... and shot his ass," I laughed...

"Yea..." she laughed as she put the camera down and began swabbing me... "Lift your neck so I can get some swabs there..."

"Okay..."

"You're all set Mrs. Osgood..."

"Thank you Tisha..." I said as I put the robe back on and headed back towards the waiting area...

# Chapter 20

"Mrs. Osgood..." Dr. Preston breathed when he saw me..."

"Yes Doctor Preston?" I asked, dreading what he was about to say...

"Your husband made it through surgery..."

"Oh thank God!" I cried as Keisha and Troy smiled...

"Mrs. Osgood..."

"What's wrong Doctor?" I asked...

"The surgery went okay but it took longer than expected..."

"Okay..."

"We had to keep stopping to stabilize him..."

"Okay..."

"His blood pressure keeps dropping..."

"Okay..."

"We had to put him in a medical coma..."

"You had to put him in a coma? I don't understand..." I said as I teared up...

"Your husband's body was fighting to get back but he lost a lot of blood and his pressure was too low – he's too weak right now to heal... if we didn't put him in a coma he might have slipped into one anyway – and he may not have come back…"

"Is my husband going to die?"

"Honestly… I don't know Mrs. Osgood…"

"What happens now?" I asked as I sat down and started crying…

"Do you believe in God?"

"Yes I do…"

"Then pray…" he said as he turned and walked towards the nurse's station…

"He's gonna be alright…" Keisha said as she rubbed my hand…

"Yes… he'll be fine…" I said as I stared off…

"Keisha… you need something to eat?" Troy asked…

"Yea – I am hungry… Beautiee… you want anything?"

"Sure… hold on a minute…" I said as I got up to go towards the nurse's station…

"Mrs. Osgood?"

"Yes Doctor Preston?"

"I gotta ask – why are you naked?" Keisha and Troy stood there with a 'No this Mutha Fucka Didn't Just Ask Her That' look on their faces…

"We were having sex…"

"You were having sex?"

"Yes…"

"I wanna make sure I'm understanding you correctly…

"Okay..."

"You were having sex when you're husband got shot?"

"Yea..."

"Is that your husband's blood on you?"

"Some of it is..."

"Oh my God – what the hell happened?"

"Long story..." I sighed.

"Do you have any clothes?"

"No..."

"So you threw on a robe, jumped in the ambulance, and came straight here – naked?"

"Yea..."

"Why didn't anyone get you any clothes?"

"There wasn't any time..."

"Are they done with you?"

"Yes..."

"Trinity!  Get Mrs. Osgood a pair of pajamas ⁻ and a shower!" he said as he started to walk away...

"Doctor Preston?"

"Yes Mrs. Osgood?"

"Can I stay?"

"You husbands in a medically induced coma – he isn't waking up anytime soon – go home – get some rest – then come back – we'll call you if anything changes..."

"Okay Doctor Preston..."

"C'mon Mrs. Osgood – let's get you in the shower and into some pajamas..."

"Keisha…. Wait for me please?" I could see Troy telling her hell no but Keisha paid him no mind…

"Okay Beautiee… but hurry up…"

"Okay… Love you…" I sang as I followed Nurse Trinity down the hall…

"Ready…" I said as I came down the hall towards them…

"Those are some cute pajamas," Troy laughed.

"Thanks Troy…" I said as I kissed him on the cheek…

"Okay – where we goin?" Keisha asked…

"Cracker Barrel…" I answered.

"I was talkin' to Troy…" Keisha laughed…

"Cracker Barrel," Troy laughed as we all walked out the hospital together and I got in their car.

"Mommy… look!" the little boy laughed as we entered Cracker Barrel…

"Shhh… that's not polite," his mother corrected…

'But Mommy – she's wearing pajamas," the little boy laughed.

"Stop laughing at her!" His mother corrected…

"Excuse me… Miss?" the little boy asked as he tugged at my pajama top…

"Yes?" I answered…

"Why are you wearing pajamas?"

"Tommy! Get over here... I'm sorry Miss," his mother said as she snatched him away from me...

"That's okay..." I said to his mother... "I'm wearing pajamas because I just got out of the hospital," I explained to Tommy.

"What happened to your clothes?"

"They got really dirty so I had to leave them there," I explained...

"Ohhh... are they gonna get washed?"

"Yea..."

"Ohhh... that's nice... bye..." he said as his mother pushed him towards their table to be seated. After we were seated, the waitress came to the table to take our orders:

"Welcome to Cracker Barrel – what can I get for you this evening?"

"Just give us one of everything on the dinner menu except pork," I answered.

"Excuse me?"

"Just give us one of everything on the dinner menu except pork!" I repeated.

"Miss... that's a lot of food... and we'll be closing soon... if you had been here about an hour earlier..."

"Just bring us one of everything you have – whatever you don't have - don't worry about it," I interrupted.

"Okay..." she said as she walked away...

"Who's eating all that food?" Keisha asked.

"We are," I said.

"We are?" Troy asked.

"You said you were hungry right?" I asked.

"Yea... but that's a lot of food," Keisha said.

"Whatever we don't eat, y'all can take home – my treat."

"Beautiee... you know this bill gonna be over $200 right?" Keisha asked.

"Here's a few of the dishes – as I said, we're about to close soon so I don't have everything..." the waitress said as she started placing the following food on the table – roast beef with mashed potatoes green beans, and carrots – country fried steak with corn – meatloaf with macaroni and cheese – parmesan crusted biscuit pot pie – country fried shrimp with fries – and farm raised catfish.

"I'll take the meatloaf and the shrimp!" I said before Keisha and Troy could say anything...

"I'm taking that country fried steak!" Troy said... "Keisha you can have all that," he laughed.

"I'm gonna tear that roast beef down... but you gonna help me eat some of this fish..." she said as she started eating...

"I'ma tear down that biscuit pot pie too," Troy said as we all continued eating...

"Thank you Lord for Keisha, Troy, and this food – AMEN!" I yelled as we all bust the food down.

"How was everything?" the waitress asked as she came over with glasses of water...

"Everything was soooooo goooooddd..." I breathed as I pulled out a $100 and slipped it in her pocket...

"Thank you miss," she said as she left the check on the table.

"Thank you Beautiee..." Troy said as we dragged ourselves away from the table...

"Thank you too..." I yawned. We all got in the car and sat quiet. We were too full to speak. When we pulled up to the house, I was afraid to get out the car... "I can't go in there..."

"You want me to go in with you?" Keisha asked.

"Keisha... let her go in there by herself..." Troy said as I started to cry... "Beautiee... we'll be right next door if you need us... but you need to do this..." Troy said as he put his arm around me...

"Okay..." I said as I walked up to the front door. When I saw the crime tape, I pulled it away from the door, went inside, and broke down crying. I cried for a while and then I remembered I had wine in the kitchen... "What the hell is this?" I said as I saw a handwritten note under the bottle of Moscato:

Beautiee,

We knew you wouldn't be able to handle seeing the house after everything that happened so while you were at the hospital with Keisha I called the Merry Maids and had them clean the house for you.

You're welcome.

Troy

"I love y'all..." I said as I took a glass of Moscato and went upstairs. "Ooohhhhh wow.... I said when I saw how clean everything was. "You can't even tell anything happened here..." I whispered as I walked over to where Bazil was shot... "Bazil...." I whispered as I lay down on the bed and cried myself to sleep.

# Chapter 21

"Good morning – Osgood Publishing – how may I help you?"

"Good morning Joselyn," I said.

"How are you Mrs. Osgood?" she greeted.

"Not too good – I need you to set up an emergency meeting with the Board of Directors – let Samuel know everyone needs to drop everything – I'll be there at 10," I said as I started getting dressed.

"I'll get right on it Mrs. Osgood – see you at 10."

"Good morning," I greeted as I walked into the Board Room and headed to the head of the table. Thank you all for coming – I'll get right to it. Last night, my husband was shot. He was rushed into emergency surgery at Milford Hospital..." I paused to gather myself as everyone gasped and whispered. I waited for the room to quiet down before I continued... "He came out of surgery but, unfortunately... he's in a coma. At this time, we don't know if he's going to make it..." I paused again to keep from crying and to also give everyone in the room time to adjust to hearing the devastating news... "Effective immediately – Samuel Logan, Vice President, will be acting President and CEO. Everything goes through him and, in turn, he will run everything by me. If there's an emergency and I cannot be reached, Samuel has the final say. Are there any questions?" I asked as Sheila Henley, CFO (Chief Financial Officer) walked in...

"Sorry I'm late..." she said as she closed the door... "What'd I miss?"

"You're fired." I stated. Everyone gasped.

"Excuse me?"

"You're fired – clean out your desk – you have one hour." Sheila exited the room in a huff, closed the door, and I continued... "Are there any questions?" No one answered. Some of the board members acknowledged what I said by shaking their head no. "Very well – thank you for coming." The board members filed out one by one. After everyone left the room, Samuel spoke...

"Mrs. Osgood?"

"Yes Samuel?"

"If you don't mind... I'd like you to reconsider your decision to fire Sheila..."

"Why?"

"We need her... she can't be easily replaced..."

"Are you saying you can't do her job in the interim?"

"I could... it's just that the quarterly reports are due and we have a responsibility to the shareholders..."

"My husband could die at any moment – and I'm here – do you really think I don't know we have a responsibility to the shareholders?"

"You're right – I'm sorry..."

"Go get Sheila," I commanded...

"Yes Mrs. Osgood..." Samuel said as he went to get Sheila..."

"Yes Mrs. Osgood?" Sheila sniffed as she sat down. I looked at her and I could tell she'd been crying...

"What's going on with you?" I asked.

"I'm sorry Mrs. Osgood... my kids..."

"Let me stop you right there!" I snapped. My husband is in the hospital in a comma – he may not make it – and I'm here – do you understand what I'm saying?"

"Yes Mrs. Osgood... sorry about your husband..."

"Samuel asked me to reconsider my decision to fire you because you're valuable and can't be easily replaced," I said as I looked at Samuel...

"Thank you Sam," she said.

"Here's what I need you to do – go home – handle whatever it is you need to handle – and come back tomorrow – but I need you to understand if life happens and you have an emergency – you are to notify us as soon as possible so we are aware – and don't ever walk in late to a board meeting again and ask what'd I miss – is that understood?"

"Yes Mrs. Osgood."

"Okay Sheila – see you tomorrow…"

"Mrs. Osgood…" Joselyn huffed out of breath as she ran into the conference room…

"Yes Joselyn – what's wrong?"

"The police are here – they asked me where you were…"

"It's okay Joselyn – get Attorney Smalls on the phone – have him meet me at the station – tell him I'm being arrested!" I yelled as Joselyn hurried… "Yes Mrs. Osgood!" she yelled as she ran down the hall…

"Mrs. Osgood?" Katina said as she walked over to me with Sergeant Chandler…

"I am…" I said as I stood up…

"We need you to come with us…" Katina said as she went to grab me by the arm…

"Excuse me!" I said as I snatched my arm away from her…

"Mrs. Osgood… please…" Sergeant Chandler asked…

"You said you need me to come with you – I'm quite capable of walking by my damn self!" I snapped as they escorted me out to the squad car.

"This way please," Katina ordered as I was escorted into the Milford City Police Department in Milford, Connecticut.

"How romantic…" I sighed.

"Excuse me?" Katina snapped…

"Well…" I laughed, "When my husband comes out of his comma… we'll be celebrating a few things… one of which will be that we both got arrested… by you!" I laughed hysterically…

"I can't wich y'all – somebody get her and process her…"

"Umm… Detective?" I asked, getting her attention…

"Yes?"

"I am under arrest… right?"

"That's correct…"

"Well…"

"What is it Mrs. Osgood?"

"Are you going to Mirandize me?"

"Oh God… is it 5:00 yet?" she sighed…

"It's always 5:00 somewhere," I laughed, enjoying the fact that she was annoyed…

"Beautiee Osgood… I'm placing you under arrest…"

"Hot Damn! What are the charges?"

"You're being charged with the attempted murder of Bazil Osgood, the murder of Sonia Santos, and the murder of Trevor Joseph…"

"Awww Shit! A Trifecta! Ahhh! Haaa! Haaa!" I laughed…

"What's going on here?" Sergeant Chandler yelled as he came down the hall…

"She thinks this is a fuckin' joke!" Katina snapped…

"That's it – get your ass over here," he said as he came towards me...

"You put your fuckin' hands on me and I'll bury your ass!" I screamed...

"Oh so you gangsta now?" he laughed...

"She's not – but you already know I am," Attorney Smalls said as he walked in...

"Look Smalls," Sergeant Chandler said...

"I'ma need you to step away from my client... have you been Mirandized yet Beautiee?"

"I was trying to do that but your client thinks this is a fuckin' joke!" Katina snapped.

"She's right – it is!" Attorney Smalls laughed, "But you don't need me to remind you that if you don't Mirandize her, you're violating her rights... and I get paid by the hour... so what we doin'?"

"Sigh..." Katina breathed as she began to give me the Miranda warning:

1. You have the right to remain silent.
2. Anything you say can and will be used against you in a court of law.
3. You have the right to an attorney.
4. If you cannot afford an attorney one will be provided for you.
5. Do you understand the rights I have just read to you?"

"I do," I said as I tried to take her hand but she snatched it away...

"With these rights in mind, do you wish to speak to me?"

"Hell no!" Attorney Smalls laughed before I could answer...

"C'mon..." Katina said as she took me for processing. Attorney Smalls met me in the attorney/client room afterwards...

"Beautiee... we need to talk..."

"I know..." I said as I sat down...

"These are some serious charges..."

"I know..."

"I'll defend you with everything I have – but I need to know everything..."

"I know..."

"This is serious... you makin' a joke out there..."

"I laugh to keep from crying..." I interrupted.

"Are you okay?"

"Hell no!"

"You need anything?"

"I need a drink..."

"The best I can do is coffee – I'll be right back," he said as he left to go get me coffee. I sat there at the table staring off into nowhere...

"How in the hell did I get here?" I asked out loud.

"Here Beautiee," Attorney Smalls said as he sat down with two cups of coffee... "Did you give them a statement?"

"Keisha and Troy did," I answered.

"Who's Keisha and Troy?"

"My neighbors... and my friends... I answered as I teared up...

"You're gonna get through this Beautiee... I gotchu..." he said as he came over to me and gave me a hug. "Let me sit here," he said as he pulled the chair up beside me..."

"If it weren't for Keisha and Troy – I'da been alone..." I said as I started to cry...

"Beautiee?"

"Yes?"

"Did they both give a statement to the police?"

"They both talked to Katina," I answered.

"Do you know what they said?"

"No..." I answered as he handed me some tissues...

"Do I need to be concerned about their statements?"

"No."

"Okay – I'll get a copy of them anyway – what happened at the hospital?"

"They swabbed me for blood samples and they took pictures..."

"Uh huh... what else?"

"They wanted to do a rape kit but I refused..."

"Did you tell them you were raped?"

"No."

"Did they ask you if you were raped?"

169

"Yes."

"What did you tell them?"

"I told them I wasn't raped."

"Okay – just so we're clear – you were not raped?"

"No – I was not raped..."

"Why the fuck did they want to do a rape kit then?"

"I'on know – maybe because I was covered in blood..."

"Hold on... let me look at these pictures... Oh shit! They didn't let you put any clothes on?"

"I didn't have any to put on..."

"Wait – you mean your friends didn't bring you any clothes?"

"There wasn't any time."

"Wait – how the fuck..."

"After Bazil was shot – they took him out on the stretcher – Troy gave me a robe to put on – I ran out the house, pushed Detective Jones out my way – and screamed for Bazil..." I explained as I cried... "Thank God they heard me screaming or I wouldn't have made it into the ambulance..." I said as I cried on his shoulder..."

"Hmmmmm... you weren't charged with assaulting an officer... I'm surprised... she actually did you a solid..."

"She didn't do shit!" I screamed... "She saw me running to get in the ambulance with Bazil and she tried to stop me – Fuckin' Bitch!"

"Calm down... I know you're upset — but that is something in your favor..." he said as he took notes... "I need to know what happened... from the beginning..."

"Okay..." I sighed... then finished my coffee... "I invited Sonia over to have sex with me so my husband could watch us and then join in..."

"Uh Huh..." he said as he wrote down what I said...

"That's all you have to say?"

"What am I supposed to say?"

"I'on know... I thought you'd be surprised..."

"I'll be surprised later... continue..."

"Okay... so Sonia agreed to come over..."

"Did Sonia know your husband would be there?"

"Yes."

"And she consented?"

"Yes."

"Okay — continue..."

"So Bazil was watching us have sex... then he joined in..."

"Was that consensual?"

"Yes."

"Did he have sex with both of you?"

"No — just me."

"So — to be clear — Bazil never touched Sonia?"

"Bazil never touched Sonia..."

"Okay — continue..."

"I saw the gun…"

"What gun?"

"I yelled for Bazil to look out but it was too late… he shot Bazil…"

"Who shot Bazil?"

"Trevor shot Bazil…" I answered as I cried…

"Okay – continue…"

"I grabbed Sonia and held her down on top of me… Trevor pointed the gun at me – but he hit Sonia instead…" I cried…

"Okay… then what happened?"

"Trevor screamed Sonia's name… and dropped the gun on the floor… and that's when I realized Sonia set us up…" I cried…

"Sonia set you up?"

"She had to! The only ones that new Sonia was invited over were me and Bazil!" I cried…

"How did Trevor get in your house?"

"I'on know!"

"Okay, okay - what happened next?"

"Trevor came over to Sonia… he started holding her… then he told me it was all my fault and she didn't deserve to die… so I picked up the gun before he could… and I shot him…"

"Oh shit!"

"He tried to shoot me first! It was self-defense!"

"I agree with you… but the defense will argue…"

"They'll argue that I should have let him pick up the gun and try again?"

"You have a point..."

"Exactly..."

"So – to be clear – Trevor was not invited to your house?"

"No."

"And – to be clear – you have no idea how Trevor got in your house?"

"No."

"Where was Trevor when he shot Bazil?"

"He was in my bedroom..."

"He was in your bedroom? And he wasn't invited?"

"No – I never, ever, invited Trevor to my house..."

"Okay Beautiee – I need to ask you something..."

"Okay..."

"Do you have any idea why Trevor would want to kill you or Bazil?"

"I know exactly why Trevor wanted us dead..."

"Why?"

"Because... Bazil and Trevor were lovers..."

"Whhhaaaattt!?"

"Bazil and Trevor were lovers – is that going to come out in court?"

"Yes..."

"Oh well..."

"So... if they were lovers... why did he want y'all dead?"

"Because... Bazil told him it was over between them..."

"Wait – Trevor wanted to kill Bazil because Bazil broke up with him... to be with you?"

"Yes..."

"Damn..." he sighed as he continued taking notes... "Is there anything else I need to know?"

"Yes..."

"Okay..."

"Bazil and Trevor have been lovers since they were in prison together..."

"I'm glad you're telling me this – that prosecuting attorney is a real Bitch – she likes to pull surprises – I'm glad we'll be one up on her ass... okay... take a look at this and tell me what you think..." he said as he pushed the pad over to me with a statement...

"I invited Sonia to my house to have sex while my husband watched. The sex was consensual. Sonia and I were having sex and my husband joined in. While we were having sex, I saw the gun and yelled for Bazil to watch out, but he couldn't move fast enough and was shot. Trevor pointed the gun at me to shoot me but because Sonia was on top of me, he shot her instead. Trevor dropped the gun on the floor, ran over to Sonia, told me it was all my fault, and Sonia didn't deserve to die. At that point, I feared for my life so I picked the gun up off the floor and shot Trevor."

"How's that?" he asked as I read it... I couldn't answer him right away... I just burst into tears...

"I'll sign it..."

"Okay – once you sign this – don't answer any questions..."

"Okay..."

"You'll be in here for tonight – but I'll get you out of here first thing tomorrow – can you make bail?"

"I'll put up my house..."

"You can't put up your house... it's in Bazil's name..."

"I said I'll put up 'MY' house..."

"Your house?"

"Yes... in Bridgeport..."

"Okay – hang in there Beautiee..." he said as he hugged me... "You ready?"

"Yea... I'm ready..." I said as I signed the statement...

"We're ready," he said after opening the door...

"Is your client ready to make a statement?" Katina asked as she sat down at the table...

"Here's her statement," he said as he pushed it to her...

"Really?" she said as she started reading it...

"That's her statement."

"This some bullshit!"

"That's up to the prosecutor."

"Whatever..." she said as she stood up... "I just want this day to be over... come with me Beautiee..."

"May I have a moment with my attorney?"

"Sigh..." she breathed as she left the room and stood outside...

"Thank you," I whispered as I gave him a hug..."

"You're welcome," he said as he tried to pull away...

"Get the surveillance..." I whispered in his ear as Katina came back into the room...

"Are you done?"

"Yes..."

"C'mon..." she said as I followed her to the holding cell.

# Chapter 22

"Good morning Your Honor," Attorney Smalls said as we went into the courtroom.

"Not really – let's get this over with – I've got a hell of a day ahead of me," she said as she sat on the Bench...

"Good morning Your Honor," the prosecuting attorney said as she stood up. "We're requesting Mrs. Osgood be held without bail due to the charges..."

"Beverly..." Attorney Smalls interrupted.

"Please address your comments to the court!" the Judge snapped.

"Yes Your Honor..." Attorney Smalls said. "Your Honor, my client's husband is in Milford Hospital in a medical comma. At this time she isn't going anywhere but the hospital. I'm requesting that she be released on her own recognizance..."

"You're kidding right?" Beverly laughed. "Attorney Smalls, you're clients been charged with the attempted murder of her husband as well as two additional murders – you can't really expect your client to get off with a slap on the wrist," she laughed.

"Thank you Your Honor," Beverly said.

"Don't thank me just yet," the judge said. "I agree the charges are serious, but I also agree that Mrs. Osgood shouldn't be held without bail. As heinous as the crimes are, Mrs. Osgood has no prior convictions – not even a parking ticket. I believe if I set bail, Attorney Smalls will ensure his client will come to court."

"Absolutely Your Honor," Attorney Smalls acknowledged.

"Very well... I'm setting bail at $200,000."

"Make sure you remind your client she can't use her husband's house to make bail," Beverly laughed as she walked out the court room...

"Don't worry about her – I'll take care of this right way – wait here," Attorney Smalls said as he went to give the Mortgage Statement, Deed, and Title information to the Bail Agent.

"Beautiee..." Keisha called as she came running into the court room...

"Hey Keisha..." I said as I got up to hug her...

"I can't stay long – I'm out to lunch – here's your clothes..."

"Thank you Keisha – I love you – kiss Troy for me..."

"I will!" she yelled as she ran out the courtroom.

"You ready?" Attorney Smalls asked as he came to take my hand...

"Yes I am!" I said as I stood up.

"Where can I take you?"

"To the ladies' room... so I can get dressed for my husband!" I answered with a smile as we walked down the hall...

"I like that," he said.

"What?"

"Seeing you smile."

"Thanks..." I said as I went into the bathroom... and broke down crying. I didn't even bother going into the stall – I just stopped right there in front of the sink – I was so happy to be out of that jumpsuit...

"Oh my God – excuse me – why didn't you use a stall?" the lady said as she came in...

"I didn't want to... I like seeing myself in the mirror..."

"Whatever," she said as she went to the bathroom, flushed the toilet, and ran out without washing her hands...

"I guess she couldn't stand the sight of me..." I laughed as I got dressed. Keisha new me well. She picked out one of my favorite outfits – the same outfit Bazil picked out for me the night he proposed. "I'm coming Bazil..." I said as I hurried out the bathroom...

"Well look at you!" Attorney Smalls said as he looked me up and down...

"Look at me!" I beamed.

"Where's the jumpsuit?"

"In the garbage!" I laughed as he took my arm and led me out the courthouse. When I saw the parking lot, I dropped down on my knees and kissed the ground. After he watched me get up, he opened his car door, made sure I was secure, and took me straight to the hospital...

"Mrs. Osgood – thank God – we've been trying to reach you!" Dr. Preston breathed.

"Sorry – I was in jail..."

"You want me to stay Beautiee?" Attorney Smalls asked.

"Please... what's wrong Doctor Preston?"

"I actually have good news..."

"Oh thank God!" I breathed.

"I'm taking your husband off the ventilator..." he said... and then paused...

"What's wrong Doctor Preston?"

"While your husband was in a comma we needed to use a stronger sedative. Normally we use Propofol but because your husband was so weak, we used Midazolam which is a Benzodiazepine. The longer the stronger sedative is used, the greater the chance of you becoming addicted to it. If we take him off the sedative too soon, he may go through withdrawal and his liver and kidney function may be impaired and we need to make sure they're at full capacity."

"Will my husband wake up?"

"Yes – he will definitely wake up – it's just going to take a bit longer. I'm going to wean him off gradually so when he does wake up, he won't go through withdrawal and his liver and kidneys will function normally."

"Thank you Doctor Preston," I said as I grabbed him into a hug and cried.

"You're welcome – I've got to get to surgery – any questions – go see Nurse Trinity!" he said as he ran down the hall...

"Well alright!" Attorney Smalls said as he hugged me...

"He's gonna be okay... he's gonna be okay..." I cried.

"I told you!"

"Yes you did!" I said as I pulled him into another hug...

"I need to get back to court – call me if you need me..." he said as he turned to leave...

"I will... thank you!"

"You're welcome!" he yelled as he left.

"Hi Trinity!" I beamed as I got to the nurses station...

"Heeeyyy! You look great!" she said as she hugged me...

"I feel great too..." I said.

"I guess you're here to see your husband..." she said as I followed her down the hall to his room.

"Hey my Thirst Quencher..." I whispered in his ear when I got up close to him... "I love you..." I said as I kissed him. I saw the monitors spike a bit, smiled, climbed in the bed with him, pulled up the covers, took his dick out of his pajamas, and played with his dick until I fell asleep.

# 3 Months Later...

"Hey my Thirst Quencher," I breathed as I plopped down in the chair. The interior designer I hired really outdid herself in making this look like a bedroom. "I've had a long day so I'm going to jump in the shower right quick... I'll be right back," I said as I stripped out of my clothes and walked into the shower...

"I wish this Bitch would realize we're not her personal maids," Thelma said as she began picking up my clothes...

"Which Bitch would you be referring too?" I asked as I came out the shower..."

"Ooohhh... Hi Mrs. Osgood... I didn't realize you were here..."

"Well now that you know I'm here, you can leave!" I snapped.

"I need to make sure your husband..."

"Get out!" I yelled as the Nurse Trinity came down the hall and into the room...

"Is everything okay in here Mrs. Osgood?" I noticed how she glared at Thelma and Thelma looked terrified. As much as I enjoyed this I started thinking Thelma might actually need her job after all...

"Yes... everything's fine," I lied. "I was just coming out of the shower and didn't realize anyone was in the room," I lied again.

"Will you be staying with your husband tonight?" she asked.

"Yes, I'll be staying tonight," I answered.

"Well, we'll give you some privacy... If you need anything at all, just let us know..." she said as she started pushing Thelma out the room...

"I sure swill," I laughed as I closed the door behind them, making sure to lock it... "Finally!" I said as I climbed into bed with Bazil and snuggled down next to him... "I miss you sooo much," I whispered in his ear as I started playing with his dick..."

"Beautiee..."

"Yes my Thirst Quencher..." I answered as I continued playing with his dick, falling asleep on Love it or List It..."

"Beautiee..." Bazil moaned again...

"Bazil?" I jumped up, climbed on top of him, and held him up...

"Beautiee..."

"Yes my Thirst Quencher..." I moaned as I sat on his dick and began riding...

"Beautiee..." he moaned as he grabbed my ass and held on tight...

"I missed this pussy..." Bazil moaned as I continued riding..."

"Oh Bazil... it's been so long..." I moaned.

"Cum with me..."

"I'm cummmmmmiiiinnnnggg..... Bazil..."

"MmmmMmmmph...MmmmMmmmph... MmmmMmmmph...

"Aaaaaggghhhhh...." I screamed as they broke the door to Bazil's room...

"Oh my God! She's trying to kill him!" Nurse Yvonne yelled as they all burst into the room...

"Oh my God... Mrs. Osgood... I'm so embarrassed..." Nurse Trinity said as she and Nurse Tisha stood in the room...

"Chille... what's a matter with you... you ain't never caught your parent's fuckin' before?" Nurse Tisha laughed as she pushed Nurse Trinity and Nurse Yvonne out of Bazil's room...

"Dr. Preston's on his way... I'll hold him at the nurse's station until you're ready for him to come in," she laughed as she closed the door...

"You didn't leave me..." Bazil whispered with tears in his eyes..."

"I made you a promise..." I said as we kissed...

"I'm so sorry Beautiee..."

"I love you my Thirst Quencher..."

"I love you too..."

"I need to get dressed... before we end up putting on another show," I laughed as I got up off of him....

"Beautiee..."

"I'll be right there my Thirst Quencher... just let me finish getting dressed...

185

"Beautiee…"

"Yes my Thirst Quencher… OH MY GOD!!! BAZIL!!!!" I screamed as Dr. Preston came rushing into the room with Nurse Trinity…

"Mrs. Osgood… we need you to leave… Dr. Preston said as he pushed past me along with Nurse Trinity…  "On three… One… Two… Three!" Dr. Preston yelled as he tried to revive Bazil with the defibrillator… "Again!  On three… One… Two… Three!" Dr. Preston yelled again as he tried again to revive Bazil with the defibrillator to no avail… "Again!"

"Dr. Preston…" Nurse Trinity whispered…

"I said again!  On three… One… Two… Three!"  Dr. Preston yelled as he tried one last time to revive Bazil with the defibrillator… "Call it…" he breathed.

"11:30 p.m." Nurse Trinity said.

"I'm so sorry Mrs. Osgood," Dr. Preston said as he put his hand on my shoulder… and I collapsed to the floor…  "Nurse… get her up here on this stretcher… STAT!"

"BAZIL?  BAZIL?  BAZIL? WHERE ARE YOU?" I cried…

"Beautiee?"

"Bazil!"

"Beautiee?  Are you really here?" he asked as tears streamed down his face…

"Yes my Thirst Quencher… I'm here," I answered, crying as we embraced…

"Beautiee… you need to go back…"

"I made you a promise…"

"Till death do us part Beautiee…"

"I never promised you that…"

"What did you promise me then?"

"When I married you… I promised you I'd love you forever…" I answered as I wrapped my arm around him…

"Yes… yes you did…" he said as we walked arm in arm towards the light…

"Beautiee…"

"Yes Lord?"

"You need to go back…"

"I can't live without Bazil…" I cried as I held on to him as tight as I could…

"Yes you can my child…"

"No… I can't…"

"Who am I Beautiee?"

"Father God," I answered lowering my head.

"Look at me Beautiee," God commanded, lifting my head up by my chin. It was so bright… all I could see where the most beautiful blue eyes… "Where is your faith? Where is your trust?"

"Right here in front of you," I whispered as I cried.

"Show me…" God commanded…

"Yes Lord," I whispered as I let go of Bazil…

"BEAUTIEE!" Bazil cried as I disappeared through the tunnel..."

"BAZIL!" God boomed.

"Yes God," Bazil whispered.

"Do you know why you're here?"

"To be honest... I thought I'd be in hell..."

"Don't try me Bazil... you still could be...

"I'm sorry God..."

"I know..."

"You know?"

"Who am I Bazil?"

"My bad... You're God..."

"You should have died a long time ago Bazil..."

"I know God..."

"Yet... you're still here... by my Grace..."

"I know..."

"You let me down Bazil..."

"I know God... I'm sorry..." Bazil said as tears streamed down his face...

"I know you are son..."

"Please God..." Bazil cried as he dropped to his knees... "Don't make Beautiee live without me..."

"She'll be just fine," God answered.

"Pleaseeeee..." Bazil cried...

"I've waited your whole life for you to come to me Bazil..."

"I know God... but I couldn't..."

"You're coming to me now..."

"I know... but this is different..."

"Because you need me?"

"Yeesss..." Bazil whispered.

"Why do you think Beautiee chose you?"

"Because I love her."

"And how do you think you wound up at that hotel?"

"Oh My God!"

"Yes Bazil... Oh Your God..."

"Thank you God...Thank you..." Bazil cried...

"You're welcome... and Bazil?"

"Yes God?"

"Don't ever hurt Beautiee again...."

"I won't God... I promise... and..."

"You never make a promise you can't keep... I know, I know," God laughed as he sent Bazil back to me...


"We've got a pulse!" Dr. Preston yelled as I opened my eyes...

"Welcome back," Nurse Trinity said as she wiped my forehead.

"I love you Bazil," I whispered as tears fell down my cheeks...

"I love you too..."

"Bazil?" I shrieked as I jumped up off the stretcher and turned to look...

"Holy shit!" Dr. Preston exclaimed... "How the fuck... Nurse Trinity - get me the neuro surgeon... now!"

"I'm on it Dr. Preston!" Nurse Trinity yelled as she ran down the hall to the nurse's station...

"What's going on?" Nurse Tisha yelled.

"He's alive! Dr. Remi...Dr. Remi!"

"What's wrong Nurse Trinity?" Dr. Remi asked as he came running...

"He's alive! He's alive!" she yelled as she grabbed him and pulled him to Bazil's room...

"Bazil Osgood!" Dr. Remi exclaimed when he saw Bazil... "Mrs. Osgood, we need to do an MRI and a CAT scan to see if your husband suffered any brain damage...

"He's fine," I sighed.

"We can't be sure of that until we run tests Mrs. Osgood...

"You may not be sure... but I am," I said as I held Bazil's hand....

"He's alive?" Nurse Yvonne asked as she came into the room...

"He's alive," Dr. Preston answered. "I still can't believe it..."

"How many miracles do you need to witness before you know God is real?" Dr. Remi asked.

"Here we go again with the bullshit..." Dr. Preston said... "This can all be explained by modern science... he probably still had brain activity after we declared him dead... I wish you'd stop trying to convince me...

"Doctor Preston?" I interrupted.

"Yes Mrs. Osgood?"

"Dr. Remi isn't trying to convince you of anything... God is," I said.

"Tell him Chille," Nurse Tisha said.

"Look Mrs. Osgood... I'm happy for you... but I'd appreciate it if you'd..."

"Doctor Preston?"

"Yes Mrs. Osgood?"

"As long as you live... you'll continue to witness miracles... whether you believe in God or not," I said matter-of-factly...

"I give up!" Doctor Preston laughed.

"C'mon... let's get your husband down to MRI," Dr. Remi said... "The sooner we get these results back, the sooner your husband can go home.

"Amen!" I said.

"C'mon Mr. Osgood – let's get you down to MRI – it'll take about an hour or so – then we'll see," Dr. Remi said as he pushed the bed down the hall towards MRI...

"I'll get the results from Dr. Remi Mrs. Osgood – if everything's okay, I'll see your husband in two weeks," Dr. Preston said as he left the room.

"You're finally going home," Nurse Trinity said.

"Yes we are – I'll be back in a bit..." I said as I ran out the hospital, jumped in the car, and headed straight home...

"Hey Beautiee — how's Bazil?" Troy asked...

"He's coming home today — I gotta go — I'll call y'all later..." I said as I opened the door and ran upstairs... "Shit — where is it?" I said out loud as I looked through the closet... "Got it!" I yelled as I grabbed his clothes, grabbed his ring, ran out the door to the car, and headed back to the hospital...

"Mrs. Osgood — you're just in time — he's good to go — but I want to see him for a follow up in 3 months..."

"Thank you Dr. Remi — where's my husband?"

"He's waiting for you in his room..."

"Thank you..." I said as I walked up to Dr. Remi... and kissed him in the mouth..."

"Mrs. Osgood... Ummm... You're welcome... I guess..." he laughed nervously...

"Mmmmmmwwwwaaa!" I said as I kissed Trinity..."

"You're welcome Beautiee..." she smiled as she hugged me...

"Thank you Tisha..." I said as I kissed her..."

"You're welcome..." she smiled... "Yvonne?"

"Yes Trinity?"

"Beautiee's taking her husband home today!"

"Congratulations!" Yvonne said as she pulled me into a hug... and I kissed her...

"Thank you Yvonne..." I laughed as Trinity and Tisha laughed with me...

"I'on know you like that for you to be kissing me..." she laughed... "Thelma..."

"Yes Yvonne?"

"Beautiee's taking her husband home today – isn't that great?"

"It sure is – I can clean his room before I go home..." she said as she kept walking down the hall past the nurse's station...

"I see you ain't rush to kiss her ass!" Yvonne laughed.

"And I won't... I'll see y'all later..." I said as I headed to Bazil's room...

"Beautiee..." he moaned as he pulled me into a kiss..."

"Hey my Thirst Quencher..." I said as I kissed him back...

"Mmmmmm... nice cologne... who's is it?" he laughed.

"It's Doctor Remi's..." I laughed as he held me.

"You must have been pretty close to him if I can smell his cologne..." he said as he kissed me again..."

"I was..." I said as I kissed him back..."

"How close were you?" he asked as we continued kissing...

"Close enough to kiss him..."

"Did you kiss him?" he moaned as he kissed me on my neck...

"Yeeesss..." I moaned as he started massaging my breasts...

"Did you kiss anyone else?" he breathed as he pulled me to him and slipped his hand in my pants...

"I kissed them all..." I moaned as he started playing with my clit...

"Hmmmmm.... just like I remembered..." he breathed as he kissed me again...

"Bazil... get dressed... so we can go home..." I said between kisses...

"Cum for me..." Bazil growled as he continued holding me with one hand and playing with my clit with the other...

"Oooohhh..." I moaned in Bazil's mouth as he covered my mouth with his while continuing to apply pressure to my clit... "Mmmmmm.... Mmmmmm.... Mmmmmm..." I moaned in his mouth as I came all over Bazil's hand.

"Mmmmmm...." Bazil moaned as he pulled his hand out my pants and licked his fingers... "Sweet..." he said as he pulled me into a kiss...

"Hurry up Bazil..." I breathed...

"Yes Beautiee..." he said seductively as he got dressed.

"Come here my Thirst Quencher..." I commanded...

"Yes Beautiee?" he asked as he walked towards me...

"With this ring... I thee wed... again..." I cried as I put the ring on his finger...

194

"I love you soooo much..." Bazil cried as he pulled me into a kiss...

"I love you too... let's go..." I said as I took him by the hand and pulled him out the room...

"Mr. Osgood – wait – your discharge papers!" Nurse Trinity yelled...

"Mail 'em!" Bazil yelled as I pulled him down the corridor and outside into the parking lot...

"Get in..." I commanded as I opened the passenger side door...

"You're driving?"

"Yes – now get in!"

"Yes Maam!" Bazil laughed as he got in and closed the door...

"Finally!" I said as I got in, closed the door, and started the car...

"Ummmmmm.... Beautiee?"

"Yes my Thirst Quencher?" I answered as I buckled up and made a beeline out the parking lot...

"You okay?"

"I'm fine – I'm just hungry – where we goin' to eat?"

"Cracker Barrel..." he said as I bust out laughing...

"What's so funny?"

"We went to Cracker Barrel... when you were in the comma..."

"We?"

"Me, Troy, Keisha..." I said as I got quiet.

"I'm sorry Beautiee..."

"I told them I wanted one of everything on the menu... but it was close to closing... so we only got six plates..." I said as I started crying...

"Beautiee... pull over..."

"No..." I said as I looked straight ahead and kept driving until we got to Cracker Barrel. Bazil kept quiet until I parked the car...

"Beautiee... wait..." he said as he touched my hand...

"Yes my Thirst Quencher?" I answered...

"C'mere..." he said as he pulled me underneath his arm and held me... "Just sit here with me..." he said as he pulled me closer to him...

"Okay..." I relented...

"I liked it when you spend the night..."

"You did?"

"Of course... you played with my dick every night... why wouldn't I like that?"

"I missed you Bazil..." I sighed.

"I missed you too... I wouldn't have made it without you..." he said as he pulled me into a kiss..."

"You wouldn't have made it without God Bazil..." I said.

"Listen to me Beautiee..."

"Okay..."

"I know God saved my life... with you..." he said as he kissed me again...

"Oh Bazil..." I said as I cried...

"Most people would have gone home after visiting hours were over... but you spent every night with me... I heard you... I felt you... I smelled your hair... I fought like hell to get back to you... and you never left me... it took 3 months... and you never left me... after everything I put you through... you never left me... I don't deserve you..." he said as he cried...

"Oh yes you do... my Thirst Quencher..." I said as I kissed his tears off his face... "And I deserve you too..." I said as I kissed him again... "Now... let's go get something to eat – because the sooner we eat... the sooner we can have dessert...

"Mmmmm... dessert..." he said as he pushed me down in the front seat and lay down on top of me...

"Bazil..."

"Yes Beautiee..." he breathed as he kissed me..."

"I'm hungry..."

"So am I..." he breathed before kissing me fully in the mouth...

"Bazil..." I said between kisses... we'll get caught..."

"It's been so long... I don't care..." Bazil said as he opened my pants and pulled them down to my ankles..."

"Oh Bazil..." I moaned as he pulled his pants down enough for me to feel his ass...

"Beautiee..." he moaned as he entered me...

"Bazil... I moaned as I kicked my pants off my ankles, spread my legs, grabbed his ass, and pushed him in deeper...

"Ugghh! Ugghh! Ugghh!" Bazil growled in my ear as he thrust harder and deeper..."

"Bazil... Bazil... Bazil..." I moaned as I put one leg up on the back of the seat...

"Gimmie that pussy... Fuuuuccckkk!!!!"

"Bazzzziiillll! I'm cuuummmmmiiinnnggg!" I screamed as I dug my fingers into his ass...

"Beautiee..." Bazil breathed as he collapsed on top of me, kissing me...

"Bazil..." I breathed in between kisses... "That was so fucking good..."

"Indeed..."

"I'm hungry..."

"You want more..."

"Yeeesss... I want more..."

"Okay... let's go eat... and when we get home... I'll give you as much as you want..."

"Promise?" I breathed as we continued kissing...

"Promise..." he breathed as he kissed me again...

"Thank God we're not parked in front of the restaurant..." I laughed as we got dressed and got out the car.

"You're back!" the waitress said as we walked in. "Are your friends joining you?"

"No... it's just us tonight..." Bazil answered as he pulled me into a kiss...

"Date night?" she asked...

"Something like that..." Bazil answered.

"Well... I hope you get my table again..." she said as she went to her section. Once we were seated she came over smiling..."I see you're in my section after all..." she laughed.

"I'll start with the grilled sirloin steak with the house salad and baked potato – she'll have the meatloaf with macaroni & cheese, string beans, and carrots..." Bazil said as he continued looking at the menu...

"Okay! Will there be anything else?" she laughed.

"Yes – you just took our dinner order – now for breakfast, we'll each have your Uncle Herschel's Favorite."

"Hash brown casserole or fried apples?" the waitress asked.

"One with the hash brown casserole – one with fried apples – we'll share..." Bazil answered.

"Will that be ham, catfish, hamburger steak, chicken tenderloins, or pork chop?" the waitress asked.

"Hhmmmmm... Beautiee... you pick..." Bazil said.

"Catfish..." I answered.

"Very well – catfish it is – may I get some drinks for you?" the waitress asked.

"Coffee for me!" I said.

"Stewart's Root Beer for me..." Bazil said as he put the menus down.

"I'll be right back with your drinks..." the waitress said as she walked away...

"God you look good..." I breathed as I took Bazil's hand across the table...

"Do I feel as good as I look?" Bazil asked seductively as the waitress brought our drinks to the table...

"Yeeesss...." I breathed...

"Oh God – this is as good as crack!" Bazil said as he started drinking his soda..."

"Poor baby... I forgot you haven't had anything to eat or drink in months...

"Exactly..." Bazil said as the waitress brought our breakfast...

"Thank you..." I said as she put the plates down...

"I'll come back to check on you before bringing your other orders – this way you'll have room on the table – if that's alright..." the waitress said.

"That's fine..." Bazil said as he took my hands across the table... "Thank God..." he whispered with tears in his eyes...

"Is he okay?" the waitress asked as she whipped tears out her eyes...

"He's fine..." I smiled.

"Okay — let's eat!" Bazil beamed as we started eating. "I missed you..." Bazil sighed as he talked to his food while eating it." I smiled as I watched him enjoy his food...

"How we 'doin over here?" the waitress asked when she came back to the table...

"Still hungry..." Bazil answered.

"I'll be right back..." she said as she went to get the rest of our food... "Will there be anything else?" she asked when she came back to the table with our plates...

"Check please..." Bazil said as he looked at me seductively. We finished eating without speaking, got up to leave, paid the check, and went out to the parking lot... "I can't wait for dessert..." Bazil whispered in my ear as he pulled me close to him...

"Neither can I..." I said as we got in the car and drove home.

# Chapter 24

When we got to the house we sat in the car for a few minutes before getting out. "You ready my Thirst Quencher?"

"Ready..." he said as we got out the car and walked up to the front door...

"You okay?" I asked as I rubbed his back...

"Yea..." he said as he opened the door and we went inside... "C'mere..." he breathed as he pulled me into a kiss...

"Mmmmmm..." I moaned... "I missed you..."

"I missed you too... come with me..." he said as he pulled me into the living room... "Take off your clothes..." he commanded...

"Yes my Thirst Quencher..." I breathed as I stripped naked and stood in front of him...

"Sit on the couch... and spread your legs..."

"Yes my Thirst Quencher..." I breathed again. Bazil stripped out of his clothes and stood in front of me without speaking. I was dripping in anticipation of what was coming next. Bazil came up close, dropped to his knees, spread my legs, placed them up on his shoulders, and dove

202

in… "Baaazzziiillll!!!" I screamed as he inserted two fingers in my pussy while licking and sucking. My legs trembled on his shoulders as he continued licking, sucking, and finger-fucking my pussy. I grabbed his head and rose up off the couch as he replaced his fingers with his tongue and I rode his face. Bazil continued to devour my pussy – so much so I could feel his teeth as he placed his hands under my ass, held me up, and sucked harder… "Ooohhh… Oooohhh… Oooohhh…" I moaned as I soaked his mouth, the couch, and his face… "Bazil… Bazil… Bazil… I'm cumming… I'm cumming… I'm cumming…. Aaaggghhhhh!" I collapsed on the couch to a degree but Bazil wouldn't let up – he held me up off the couch, spread my legs wider with his head, and sucked all my squirting… "Damn Bazil… Shit…" I breathed as he slowed down a bit but continued licking and sucking…

"Mmmmmm…" he moaned as my orgasm subsided… "Sweet…" he said as he stood up, got on top of me, and began thrusting inside me… standing back up…

"Oooohhhh…." I moaned as he started thrusting harder and deeper…

"Yeeesss…. Gimmie that pussy…" he growled…

"Fuck me Bazil…" I moaned. Bazil pushed me down on my back, climbed on top of me, and did as he was told…

"Is this what you want?" he growled as he fucked me harder...

"Bazzzziilll!" I screamed...

"Say it!" he growled...

"Fuck meeeeee!" I screamed as I came again...

"Uugghh! Uugghh! Uugghh! Uugghh! Uugghh!" Bazil collapsed on top of me and we both just lay there kissing... "I missed you Beautiee..."

"I missed you too..."

"I can tell..." he laughed as we continued kissing...

"Bazil..."

"Yes Beautiee..."

"Don't ever leave me again..."

"Never..."

"You promise?"

"Yeesss... I promise..."

"I love you my Thirst Quencher..."

"I love you too... let's go upstairs..." he said as he got up off me and picked up his clothes...

"Okay..." I said as he helped me up off the couch, picked up my clothes, and I followed him upstairs to our bedroom...

"Hmmmmm... this isn't the same room..." he said as he entered...

"I had it re-decorated..."

"Why?"

"I wanted it to look just like the hotel room where you proposed to me..." I answered as we sat on the bed...

"Aww..." he said as he pulled me into a kiss... "I need to ask you something Beautiee...

"Okay..."

"What happened?"

"You don't remember?"

"It's a bit fuzzy..."

"Tell me what you remember..."

"What happened Beautiee?"

"Tell me what you remember..."

"Beautiee..."

"Yes Bazil..."

"Tell me... please..."

"I need to know what you remember Bazil..." I pleaded with tears in my eyes...

"Don't cry Beautiee..." he said as he kissed me... I know it was bad... but I need to know..."

"Okay... let's get dressed..." I said as I tried to get my clothes...

"Let's not... tell me..."

"You were shot..."

"Where?"

"In here..."

"In this room?"

"Yes..."

"What happened?"

"I invited Sonia over... like you asked..."

"I asked you to invite Sonia over?"

"Yes..."

"Hmmmmm... why?"

"Because you wanted to watch us have sex..."

"Ohhh! So did she come over?"

"Yes..."

"Did you have sex?"

"Yes..."

"Was I watching?"

"Yes..."

"Where was I?"

"You were in the closet..."

"I was?"

"Yes..."

"Did I come out the closet?"

"Yes..."

"What happened after I came out the closet?"

"You joined us over there..." I said as I pointed to the area beneath the night stand...

"Did I participate?"

"Yes..."

"So... I was in the closet... I came out... I stood over there... and I was shot?"

"You came out the closet... you had sex with me while I was doing Sonia..."

"Oh... I see..."

"Then when Sonia started doing me... you came over here so you could put your dick in my mouth..."

"Oooohhh..."

"Trevor shot you..." I whispered. Bazil didn't say anything. He just sat there for a few minutes...

"You're lying..."

"No Bazil..."

"Trevor loves me... he would never hurt me..."

"Trevor shot you Bazil..."

"Are you sure?" he asked as he grabbed me by my shoulders...

"Bazil... you're scaring me..."

"Trevor was here? While we were having sex?"

"Yes..."

"And he shot me?"

"Yes..."

"Why?"

"Because you told him it was over between you..."

"Wait a minute... I'm starting to remember... you caught us together... you caught us... you left me... then you came back..."

"That's right..."

"How did Trevor get in here?"

"Sonia set us up..."

"Sonia?"

"Yes..."

"Are you sure?"

"Yes..."

"How do you know?"

"I saw the gun..." I answered as I started to cry... "I yelled for you to look out but you didn't move fast enough... and he shot you..."

"Beautiee... it's okay... I'm here..." Bazil said as he held me...

"No it isn't!" I yelled... "He tried to kill me too!"

"What did you say?"

"After he shot you... he pointed the gun at me... I pulled Sonia down on top of me... but Sonia got hit... he dropped the gun and came over to Sonia... he told me it was all my fault... he said Sonia didn't deserve to die..." I cried...

"Sonia? Sonia and Trevor?"

"I picked up the gun... I told him she deserved to die and so did he... and I shot him..." I cried...

"I'm so sorry... please don't cry..." Bazil said as he started crying too...

"Katina arrested me..."

"What?!"

"I was charged with attempted murder, murder, and murder!"

"Beautiee... Nooooo....."

"My bail was set at $200,000! I put up my house to make bail!"

"Why Trevor Why?" Bazil cried as he continued to hold me and we cried together...

"Because you chose me Bazil..."

"Damn right I chose you... I love you sooo much... you went through this all alone..."

"I wasn't alone..."

"You weren't alone?"

"Keisha and Troy were here when the paramedics came..." I said as I started crying again... "Keisha rode with me to the hospital... she never left my side..."

"I'm sorry..." Bazil said, crying as he held me...

"When Trevor shot you I screamed... Keisha told Troy to break the door down... they both came running upstairs... they saw us naked... I was covered in blood... you were lying on the floor over there... Sonia was on the bed... Trevor was over there..."

"I'm sorry... I'm sorry..."

"They stayed with me at the hospital... they took me to eat... they even paid to have the house cleaned so when I came home it looked as if nothing happened – I don't know what I would have done without them..."

"I'm sorry..."

"I was naked, covered in blood – they swabbed me to get samples – they even wanted to do a rape kit!"

"Oh my God... No... Please tell me..."

"Trevor didn't rape me... he never touched me..."

"Oh thank God..."

"I went to work to let everyone know what happened... Samuel has been Acting President in your absence..."

"I love you soooo much... you went through all this... you never left me... you held me down..." Bazil said as he broke down crying...

"Smalls held us both down..."

"Smalls?"

"Yea..." Bazil stopped crying and started to smile.

"I owe him my life... he held you down... let's get dressed..." Bazil said as he started getting dressed...

"I thought you didn't want to?"

"I didn't... but I need to go see Smalls..."

"Can't you go later... please?" I pleaded as I looked up at him... tugging on his pants to bring him closer to me...

"I guess I can go see him later..." he said as I loosened his pants, dropped them to the floor along with his boxers, and pulled him closer to my mouth... "Beautiee..." he moaned as I began sucking his dick. I grabbed his ass and pushed him deeper into my mouth as he grabbed my head. I relaxed my throat as he closed his eyes, leaned his head back, and fucked my mouth...

"Mmmmmm..." I moaned so he could feel the vibration...

"Shiiittt... that's it... take this dick... suck it..." I began alternating between pulling his dick all the way out my mouth and deep throating him as he watched...

"I missed you my Thirst Quencher..." I said as I pulled his dick out my mouth and deep throated him again...

"I can tell..." Bazil breathed, smiling as he watched me enjoy pleasing him...

"Cum in my mouth..." I commanded...

"Oh shit... fuck... that's it... suck it... suck it... Ugghh! Ugghh! Ugghh!" I swallowed every bit and continued sucking as Bazil started shaking... "Easy Beautiee... I'm a bit sensitive..."

"Mmmmm..." I moaned as I continued sucking a little softer...

"You want more?" he breathed...

"Yes... I want more..."

"Gimmie a minute... I need to re-energize... I'm a little weak... you sucked the shit outta me..."

"I couldn't help it..." I said as I continued sucking his dick softly..."

"Let's get in bed..."

"Okay..." I said as I moved back on the bed and pulled him down on top of me...

"I love you..." Bazil said as he kissed me...

"I love you too..."

"I need some sleep..." he yawned as he lay beside me...

"So do I..." I yawned as I snuggled underneath him and we fell asleep.

# Chapter 25

"Good morning... we both need to get dressed..." Bazil said as he kissed me awake...

"Come back to bed..." I moaned...

"We need to go see Smalls..." Bazil said as he climbed on top of me...

"I need to eat..." I moaned as we started kissing...

"Are you hungry?" Bazil asked as he thrust himself inside me...

"Yeesss... I'm hungry!" I moaned as Bazil thrust harder and deeper...

"I'm a bit hungry myself..." Bazil breathed in my ear before he started kissing my neck...

"Bazil..." I moaned as I spread my legs, grabbed his ass, and pushed him in deeper....

"Mmmmm..." Bazil moaned into my mouth as he kissed me fully....

"Mmmmm... Mmmmm... Mmmmm..." I moaned back into his mouth as I was cumming...

"Mmmmmph! Mmmmmph! Mmmmmph!" Bazil moaned into my mouth before collapsing down on top of me. We continued kissing for a few moments until Bazil spoke... "We need to get dressed..." he said between kisses...

"No..." I breathed as he tried to get up and I pulled him back down on top of me...

"Beautiee..."

"Yes my Thirst Quencher..."

"We need to go see Smalls..."

"Please... Don't make me go..." I pleaded as we continued kissing...

"Beautiee..."

"No..." I whispered as I started to cry...

"Beautiee..." Bazil whispered as he kissed my tears...

"I just want this to be over..."

"I know..."

"I'm tired Bazil..."

"I know... I'm sorry..." Bazil whispered as he started to cry...

"Don't cry Bazil..." I whispered as I kissed his tears and his lips...

"I love you so much Beautiee..." he whispered as he continued crying...

"I love you too... please don't cry..."

"I'll stop if you stop..."

"Okay... I'll go see Smalls..."

"Okay... let's get dressed before you change your mind..."

"Mmmmm... you keep kissing me like this and we're not going anywhere..." I breathed as I rolled him over and slid down between his legs...

"Beautiee... No..."

213

"Wait a minute..." I laughed... "Did you just say no to me?"

"I guess I did..." he laughed...

"Remember that..." I laughed as I jumped up, ran to the bathroom, and jumped in the shower...

"Where do you think you're going?" Bazil laughed as he turned me around and pulled me into a kiss...

"To... see... Smalls..." I moaned as he put his hand between my legs...

"I'm sorry I told you no..." he breathed as I started playing with his dick...

"Apology not accepted!" I laughed as I threw the loofah full of soap at him...

"Oh... okay... it's like that is it?" he laughed as he grabbed me, shoved me into the corner, and held me against the wall with his body... "Please... accept... my... apology..." he breathed between kisses...

"No... I won't..." I laughed.

"Okay..." he relented as he pushed me down on the bench and brought his dick to my mouth...

"My... Thirst... Quencher..." I moaned as I put his dick in my mouth and began sucking it...

"Yesss..."

"Don't... you... ever... tell... me... no... again..." I breathed as I sucked his dick... "Do... you... understand... me... my... Thirst... Quencher?"

"Yeeesss..." Bazil moaned...

"Who's... dick... is... this?"

"Yoouuurrrsss..."

"That's... right... now... give... it... to... me..."

"Oh shit... fuck... Aggghhh!"

"Mmmmm..." I moaned as I continued sucking Bazil's dick until his orgasm subsided...

"Damn..." he breathed as he pulled me up from the bench, pulled me close to him, and kissed me hard. I grabbed the loofah with one hand, soaped it up with the other, and washed the back of Bazil's body as he held me. Bazil loosened his grip a little as I washed the front of his body, never letting go of me. When I was done he took the loofah as I held onto him, soaped it up, and pulled me into a kiss as he washed the back of my body. I loosened my grip a little as he started washing the front of my body...

"Oh Bazil..." I moaned as he began kissing my neck, then sucking my breasts as he washed them... "Bazil..." I moaned as he began washing my pussy, swirling the loofah around my clit... "Mmmmm... Mmmmm...." I moaned as Bazil dropped the loofah and began fucking me with his fingers...

"Now I'm thirsty..." Bazil growled as he sat on the bench and dove between my legs...

"Bazil... Bazil... Bazil..." I moaned as he licked and sucked my pussy while finger-fucking me...

"Mmmmm... he moaned as I started cumming and my legs started shaking...

"Bazil! I'm cumming! I'm cumming!" Bazil slowed down but continued to lick, suck, and fuck me with his fingers as my orgasm subsided. When he was finished he stood up, pulled me into a kiss, and whispered in my ear...

"Do you accept my apology now?"

"Yes my Thirst Quencher..." I breathed... "Yeeessss..."

# Chapter 26

"Well it's about Damn time!" Smalls laughed as he grabbed Bazil into a hug.

"I love you brother..." Bazil said as he kissed Smalls in the mouth...

"I love you too man..." Smalls said as they embraced for a moment...

"Ahem?" I exclaimed to get their attention...

"Beautiee!" Smalls said as he grabbed me into a hug and tried to kiss me...

"Oh no – don't act like you love me now!" I laughed as I pushed him away...

"C'mere you!" he said, grabbing me into a kiss before I could object...

"Watch it!" Bazil laughed.

"Sit down y'all – we have a lot to go over..." Smalls said as he got serious...

"What's going on Smalls?" Bazil asked...

"Let's start with Beautiee..."

"Okay..." I sighed...

"Beautiee – we got a hold of the surveillance footage..."

"Surviellance?" Bazil asked...

"Bazil... be quiet... this isn't about you... yet..." Smalls said...

"Go 'head man..." Bazil said...

"Beautiee – we got a hold of the surveillance..."

"That's good..." I said...

"Not really..."

"Why not?"

"It shows Trevor just opened the door and walked right in – Katina's going to present it to the D.A. as if he was invited..."

"He wasn't fucking invited!" Bazil growled.

"I know that Bazil – but this is about Beautiee... please..."

"I didn't invite him..." I said as I started to cry...

"I swear to God – if that mutha fucka wasn't already dead I'd fuckin' kill him!" Bazil yelled.

"Damnit Bazil – shut the fuck up!" Smalls yelled.

"Do you know who the fuck you're talking too?" Bazil growled.

"I'm talking to Bazil J. Osgood – known felon – convicted murder – person of interest in the disappearance of Beautiee's ex-husband, Billie and also person of interest in the disappearance of your former employee, MaryJane LaRue – but I'm also talking to my brother and my friend – now shut the fuck up! Please!"

"I'm sorry..." Bazil sighed.

"Beautiee – as long as you tell me you didn't invite him that's what I'll present to the D.A. – but I have to be honest – Beverly is going to try to convince the judge that you didn't kill him in self-defense – you killed him because you were jealous of his relationship with Bazil..."

"Are you telling us my wife can be convicted?" Bazil asked...

"Beverly will send it to the Grand Jury – it's circumstantial – but..."

"But what Smalls?"

"It's you Bazil..." Smalls sighed...

"Beautiee... I'm sorry..." Bazil whispered as tears streamed down his face...

"Don't cry Bazil..." I said as I took his hand and cried with him. Smalls handed us a box of tissues after taking some for himself...

"I wish I never knew Trevor..." Bazil cried...

"I wish you never knew him either..." I cried...

"Beautiee... I need to ask you something..." Smalls said...

"Yes?"

"What happened to your ex-husband?"

"I have no idea..."

"Beautiee... they have the surveillance..."

"What surveillance?"

"They have the surveillance from the hotel..." Bazil answered.

"Is that true?" I cried.

"Yes Beautiee…" Smalls answered.

"Why?"

"Katina has a bug up her ass when it comes to Bazil – they've been watching him ever since he got out of prison…" Smalls explained.

"Beautiee had nothing to do with that…" Bazil said…

"Don't say another fuckin' word Bazil…" Smalls growled…

"I said Beautiee had nothing to do with that…" Bazil repeated…

"What are you telling me Bazil?" Smalls asked…

"I'm not telling you anything…"

"Are they going to find anything Bazil?"

"There's nothing to find…"

"Bazil… you know you can tell me anything… right?"

"Yes Smalls…"

"You know our conversations are privileged right?"

"Yes Smalls…"

"Okay… as your attorney… I'm asking you… is there anything you need to tell me?"

"Yes…"

"Damn… I knew it… go 'head…"

"Billie was in prison with us…"

"You… and Trevor?"

"Yes…"

"Okay – good – continue…"

"I never trusted that mutha fucka... but he was very close to Trevor..."

"How close?"

"One night I heard Trevor screaming for help... Billie owed a debt... and he was trying to pay that debt with Trevor..." Bazil said as he started tearing up...

"You loved him... didn't you?"

"Yes..."

"Damn... I hope this doesn't come out in court... but it probably will..."

"There's more..."

"What else?" Smalls asked as he threw up his hands...

"Billie told Trevor all about Beautiee..."

"So what?"

"So he told Trevor that he was going to get revenge on her for leaving him as soon as he got out of prison..."

"So that's what happened at the hotel?"

"Yes..."

"Damn... so you knew who Beautiee was all along..."

"No..."

"You didn't know who Beautiee was?"

"I met Beautiee that night at the hotel... and I fell in love with her..." Bazil said as he took my hand...

"Hmmmmm... this is hearsay... but it might help..."

"How?" I asked...

"Maybe Trevor wanted to get revenge on Billie... for what happened in prison..."

"Maybe..." Bazil smiled...

"And maybe... Trevor wanted Bazil out of the way... so he could have Beautiee all to himself..."

"Maybe..." Bazil smiled again...

"I can't prove it... but they can't either..." Smalls smiled... "Thank you for telling me Bazil..."

"You're welcome..." Bazil smiled...

"Bazil... there's something you need to do..."

"What's that?"

"You need to tell Beautiee the truth..."

"What's he talking about Bazil?" I asked with tears in my eyes...

"I can't..." Bazil whispered...

"Bazil... please..." I whispered...

"I'm scared..." Bazil whispered as he cried...

"Don't cry Bazil..." I said as I kissed his tears...

"Please don't leave me Beautiee..." he cried...

"Never..." I said as I pulled him into a kiss...

"Promise?"

"Promise..."

"I killed her..."

"Who?"

222

"Janet..."

"Who's Janet?"

"My first wife..."

"Why Bazil?"

"Because she tried to leave me..."

"Like me?"

"Yes..."

"So... that night... we're you going to kill me too Bazil?"

"Beautiee... I didn't mean to kill Janet... it was an accident..."

"Like me?"

"She hit her head on the counter... I begged her not to leave me..."

"So that night... when you threw me into the counter... and I stabbed you... what were you planning to do to me Bazil? Huh?"

"I wasn't planning to kill you... I swear..."

"How can I be sure?" I whispered with tears in my eyes...

"I wasn't trying to kill you Beautiee... I swear... please believe me..." he said as he broke down crying...

"What were you planning to do Bazil?" I asked with tears in my eyes...

"I was planning to lock you up in the house until I could convince you to stay..." Bazil cried as he dropped to his knees and held me by my legs...

"Okay..."

"So you believe me?" Bazil asked as he got up and sat beside me...

"Yes Bazil... I believe you..."

"I love you so much..."

"I love you too..."

"Hold up!" Smalls interrupted...

"I need to tell you something..." I said.

"Yes Beautiee?" Smalls asked...

"I'm the one responsible for the disappearance of MaryJane LaRue...

"Oh shit! Y'all some gangstas! Le'me write this shit down!" Smalls said as he grabbed a pad and started scribbling...

"I went to see Bazil at work..."

"Uh huh..." Smalls said as he kept scribbling..."

"I walked into Bazil's office..."

"Uh huh..."

"And I caught him fuckin' the Bitch!"

"What?! Damn Bazil! What the fuck is wrong with you?" Smalls yelled. Bazil didn't say anything... he just went along with my story...

"Bazil jumped up when he saw me..."

"Uh huh..." Smalls said as he kept scribbling...

"And I went over to her, snatched her up by her fuckin' hair, dragged her ass to the door, and bounced her out on her ass! Right Bazil?"

"Yea..." Bazil acknowledged...

"Uh huh..." Smalls said, still scribbling...

"I told her she was fired – and I also told her if I ever caught her near my husband again I would fuckin' kill her! Isn't that right Bazil?"

"Yea..." Bazil acknowledged...

"So... to be clear... you caught your husband cheating on you with her – you told her she was fired – and you threatened to kill her if you ever saw her near your husband again?" Smalls asked.

"That's right..." I answered...

"Where there witnesses?" Smalls asked...

"Joselyn Logan..."

"Who's she?"

"Bazil's new Personal Assistant."

"She witnessed this?"

"Yes..."

"And she heard you threaten MaryJane LaRue?"

"Yes..."

"That might be a problem..."

"For who?"

"For you – she'll be called to testify..."

"So what?"

"Beautiee – you just admitted you threatened her..."

"Yes I did – and there isn't a woman anywhere in the world – including the D.A. – that will blame me or convict me for threatening to kill the woman I caught fucking my husband!" I said matter-of-factly.

"Hmmmmmm… you're probably right… so… just to be clear… Bazil – you had nothing to do with the disappearance of MaryJane LaRue?"

"No… I didn't…" Bazil answered…

"And… to be clear… you haven't seen her - or been with her since she was fired?"

"Hell no!" Bazil answered…

"Okay – this is good – I'll keep you posted – Beautiee – could you give us some privacy?" Smalls asked.

"Uummmmm… okay…" I hesitated as I got up to go sit outside in the waiting area.

"Help yourself to coffee… or anything else you want…" he said as I opened the door to leave…

"Okay – thanks…" I said as I closed the door. "I guess they want to catch up…" I said out loud as I made myself some coffee, sat down on the sofa, and made myself comfortable. After 30 minutes or so I got up and went to see what was going on… "Guys?" I said as I knocked on the office door… "Hello?" I said as I opened the door and went inside… "Bazil…" I whispered as I tried to wake him… and then I saw the empty bottle of Jack Daniels and the two empty glasses… "Well damn!" I laughed… "What the hell were you celebrating?" I said out loud as I picked up the empty bottle of Jack Daniels, put it in the trash, and put the empty glasses on the table… "Oh shoot… is that Bazil's phone?" I asked out loud as I looked around… "Oh shoot –

that's Small's phone!" I said as I took it out of his pocket and answered it... "Attorney Smalls office – may I help you?"

"This is Katina – is Smalls available?"

"He's out right now – may I have him return your call?"

"Yes please..."

"May I tell him what it's in reference to?"

"Tell him Beautiee Osgood – urgent."

"I sure will..." I said as I hung up...

"Beautiee..." Bazil yawned as he tried to sit up... "Oh damn – my head hurts – I'm gonna be sick!" Bazil yelled as he stumbled to the toilet just in time... "Uuuggghhh!" I heard as everything came up and into the toilet...

"Damn... what's that smell?" Smalls said as he woke up... "Oh shit – move Bazil!" he yelled as he hit the toilet just in time... "Oh God – I'm gonna die!" he moaned...

"Serves your ass right!" Bazil laughed. I watched them both in the bathroom as Bazil used the mouthwash and then Smalls.

"Next time we'll go out to eat – then we'll drink!" Smalls sighed...

"There won't be a next time!" Bazil laughed...

"Hey Beautiee... you alright?" Smalls asked...

"I'm fine," I laughed...

"Shit – where's my phone..."

"Here..." I said as I handed him his phone...

"Oh shit — Katina called..."

"I know..."

"You answered my phone?"

"Yes..."

"What she say?"

"She said please call her regarding Beautiee Osgood — urgent..."

"Damn — that's not good — I gotta go — I'll call you!" Smalls yelled as he ran out the office...

"C'mon Bazil..." I sighed as I opened the door to Smalls' office so we could leave...

"We need to get down to the station..." Bazil said...

"No we don't!" I yelled

"Smalls said..."

"I heard what Smalls said! I'm going home — with you — end of discussion!"

"Okay Beautiee..." Bazil said as he kissed me... "Whatever you want..."

"Right now I want you..."

"That's fine with me..." Bazil said as he kissed me again.

www.ingramcontent.com/pod-product-compliance
Lightning Source LLC
Chambersburg PA
CBHW072231170626
46813CB00003B/1166